Cambridge E

GW01451475

Elements in Beckc
edited by
Dirk Van Hulle
University of Oxford
Mark Nixon
University of Reading

PILGRIM'S GRESS: THE BECKETT WALK

Andre Furlani
Concordia University

CAMBRIDGE
UNIVERSITY PRESS

![CAMBRIDGE UNIVERSITY PRESS]

Shaftesbury Road, Cambridge CB2 8EA, United Kingdom

One Liberty Plaza, 20th Floor, New York, NY 10006, USA

477 Williamstown Road, Port Melbourne, VIC 3207, Australia

314–321, 3rd Floor, Plot 3, Splendor Forum, Jasola District Centre, New Delhi – 110025, India

103 Penang Road, #05–06/07, Visioncrest Commercial, Singapore 238467

Cambridge University Press is part of Cambridge University Press & Assessment, a department of the University of Cambridge.

We share the University's mission to contribute to society through the pursuit of education, learning and research at the highest international levels of excellence.

www.cambridge.org
Information on this title: www.cambridge.org/9781009507462

DOI: 10.1017/9781009180689

First published 2025

A catalogue record for this publication is available from the British Library

ISBN 978-1-009-50746-2 Hardback
ISBN 978-1-009-18069-6 Paperback
ISSN 2632-0746 (online)
ISSN 2632-0738 (print)

Pilgrim's Gress: The Beckett Walk

Elements in Beckett Studies

DOI: 10.1017/9781009180689
First published online: February 2025

Andre Furlani
Concordia University

Author for correspondence: Andre Furlani, andre.furlani@concordia.ca

Abstract: Walking is a governing trope and structure as well as theme in Samuel Beckett's work; a narrative and performance figure, a framing device and a material practice. Walking begins as a plot device and motif, expands into a compositional principle and culminates in a gressive ontology of unmotivated onwardness; peripatetic coming and going as the basis of human possibility and ethical value. His texts increasingly enact stylistically the interpenetration of mind and body in the peripatetic situation, which develops from a solipsistic evasion into an exercise in shared acquiescence in transitory being. Walking in Beckett can be palliative, epistemic, a task, a regression, a repudiation or a mourning regimen, but most innovatively it comes to serve as an ontological warrant, affirming a finite, exposed, contingent embodiment. The Beckett walk is examined with reference e.g. to cognitive and performativity theory, environmental and mobility studies, and cultural and literary history.

This Element also has a video abstract:
www.cambridge.org/EIBS_Furlani_abstract

Keywords: Beckett, walking, fiction, drama, mobility

ISBNs: 9781009507462 (HB), 9781009180696 (PB), 9781009180689 (OC)
ISSNs: 2632-0746 (online), 2632-0738 (print)

Contents

Figure 1 *Quadrat II*, Süddeutscher Rundfunk (1981).

Introduction: 'On!'

'My work is a matter of fundamental sounds (no joke intended) made as fully as possible', Samuel Beckett publicly declared when *Endgame* was staged in New York in 1957 (Beckett, 1983, 109; see Beckett and Schneider, 1998, 24). Among the most fundamental of these, resounding off the *fundus* (soil, ground) itself, yet so common and inconspicuous as to be inaudible, is the footstep. 'One should always hear Vladimir's feet', he instructed director Alan Schneider for the American premier of *Waiting for Godot* (Beckett and Schneider, 1998, 6; Beckett, 2011, 586). In a 1957 letter he approved a recording of *Endgame* that captures 'Clov's feet' (Beckett, 2014b, 229). Clov's blind taskmaster Hamm attends to it, irritably asking his menial as he approaches the door of potential escape, 'what's wrong with your feet? Clov: My feet? Hamm: Tramp, tramp! Clov: I must have put on my boots. Hamm: Your slippers were hurting you? Clov: I'll leave you' (Beckett, 1958c, 57–8). These boots are made for walking, so this is no negligible detail, nor is Beckett's substitution of the original 'On dirait un regiment de dragons' (Beckett, 1957, 79) to accentuate the thud ('Tramp, tramp!') rather than concoct an analogy. Such resonant walking forestalls the effacement threatening his figmentary characters, such as May in *Footfalls*: '*Steps: clearly audible rhythmic tread*', a stage direction indicates (Beckett, 1984, 239). Tread individuates even the anonymous players of *Quad*: 'Footsteps: Each has his own particular sound' (292; see Figure 1). The compulsive tread of the loner is enumerated in ... *but the clouds* ... : '*He advances five steps*' (261, 262). In *Company*, the loner tabulates 'the growing sum' of his steps (Beckett, 1996, 9). Charles Lock observes that 'the imagination seldom shows consideration for the needs and the demands of the feet' (Lock, 2024, 129). Beckett's literary imagination is a paramount modern exception.

'And of course he did a lot of walking', Barbara Bray wrote in an uncompleted memoir of Beckett. 'As a lot of writers have said, their best ideas come when they walk. He was a great walker' (Bray qtd in Kedzierski, 2011, 894). The equation between walking and composing was familiar to Beckett from Jean-Jacques Rousseau, who in *The Confessions* states:

> Never did I think so much, exist so vividly, and experience so much, never have I been so much myself – if I may use that expression – as in the journeys I have taken alone and on foot. There is something about walking which stimulates and enlivens my thoughts. When I stay in one place I can hardly think at all; my body has to be on the move to set my mind going. (Rousseau, 1953, 157–8)

The Victorian writer and Alpinist Leslie Stephen writes in 'In Praise of Walking' that 'the true walker' is one 'to whom the muscular effort of the legs is subsidiary to the "cerebration" stimulated by the effort; to the quiet musings and imaginings which arrive most spontaneously as he walks, and generate the intellectual harmony which is the natural accompaniment to the monotonous tramps of his feet' (Stephen, 1948, 21; see Figure 5).

Robert Walser declares in the 1917 story 'The Student': 'Wandering, yes, that was the student's joy! Marching was for him something like a musical pleasure. Thinking and walking, musing and pacing, composing and striding were related to one another' (Walser, 1985, 211; my translation). Beckett's stablemate at the German publishing house Suhrkamp, Thomas Bernhard, recounts in *Walking* (*Gehen*) the stroll of two friends discussing how 'walking and thinking are quite similar concepts': 'Walking and thinking stand in an uninterruptedly intimate relationship to one another, says Oehler. The science of walking and the science of thinking are fundamentally a single science' (Bernhard, 1971, 85–6; my translation). Beckett at times programmatically attempted to practice this science. His German sojourn of 1936–7 was largely cast as a walking cure for depression and attendant writing block (see e.g. Hartel, 2006). He walked the vast Ohlsdorf cemetery on the periphery of Hamburg explicitly for poetic impetus, which however materialised only a decade later, transmuted as the beginning of the story 'Premier amour' ('First Love'). 'I am taking things very easy here', he wrote from Dublin on 25 April 1946, 'writing a little and walking a lot' (Beckett, 2011, 29). Walking to write, he wrote about walking extensively during what would become his most fertile period. 'Walked many miles &

written a few lines', he wrote while composing *Company* at his Ussy retreat some thirty years later, entering his final fertile period (Beckett, 2016, 475).

The Beckett walk begins as a motif of respite, refusal or evasion and culminates in a compositional practice that encompasses an ontology of flux. The walk advances from a subject of representation to a rhetorical trope that presents the mind's entwinement in bipedal movement; a shift from contingent pedestrian passage to stylistic determinant. Practice and notation merge, body and mind also. The basis of cognition is the kinaesthetic situation of the body – *basis* literally meaning not *ground* but *steps* along a ground. Whereas his early fictional alter ego Belacqua goes for a walk and the slacker of 'The End' walks simply to go, increasingly Beckett will take textuality itself for a walk. *The Unnamable* urges itself: 'Keep going, going on, call that going, call that on' (Beckett, 1958a, 3). Dromomania impels graphomania – twinned compulsions to walk and to write – as in Henry's opening word as he stamps across the stone beach of *Embers*: 'On. [*Sea. Voice louder.*] On! [*He moves on. Boots on shingle*]' (Beckett, 1984, 93). On Beckett's version of 'Dover Beach', Henry directs his step and likewise this radio play, peripatetic and textual operations coinciding.

Like Beckett, his characters do a lot of walking, indeed it is the inveterate occupation of a host of them. Among others there is Belacqua pummelled with his own walking stick in *More Pricks than Kicks*, Watt's spastic walk, the vagrants of the early *nouvelles*, Molloy on exhilarating crutches, Estragon hobbling in pinching tattered shoes and Lucky trudging valises in *Waiting for Godot*, Maddie grunting down the country road in *All That Fall*, Pim crawling in *How It Is*, O (the Object) evading a predatory lens in *Film*, May pacing before her mother's bedroom in *Footfalls*, the landloping wretch in . . . *but the clouds* . . ., the synchronised pacers of *Quad*, the widow in the pasture of *Ill Seen Ill Said*, man and child hand in hand in *Worstward Ho*. As Thomas Browne discerned in the human stride the quincunx that formed the basic morphology of creation (see Browne, 1896, 126–7), so Beckett seizes on the elementary activity of the step (see Figure 2).

Though Beckett's characters long to take refuge in the mind, they usually take root instead at the soles. Beckett seizes on the improbable, hazardous, highly expressive yet curiously enigmatic mechanics of walking, which had been the object of close yet inconclusive scientific investigation over the previous century by the brothers Weber, Christian Braun and Otto Fischer, Étienne-Jules Marey and Eadweard Muybridge (see Figures 2, 3 and 9). The research into a standard human gait was foiled by what Andreas Mayer calls the cultural and personal interplay of mechanical, semiotic and poetic registers in this activity (see Mayer, 2020, 99–141). Treatises from the seventeenth century on had defined walking as an interrupted topple. 'Walking, then, is a perpetual falling with a perpetual self-recovery', Oliver Wendell Holmes stated in 'The

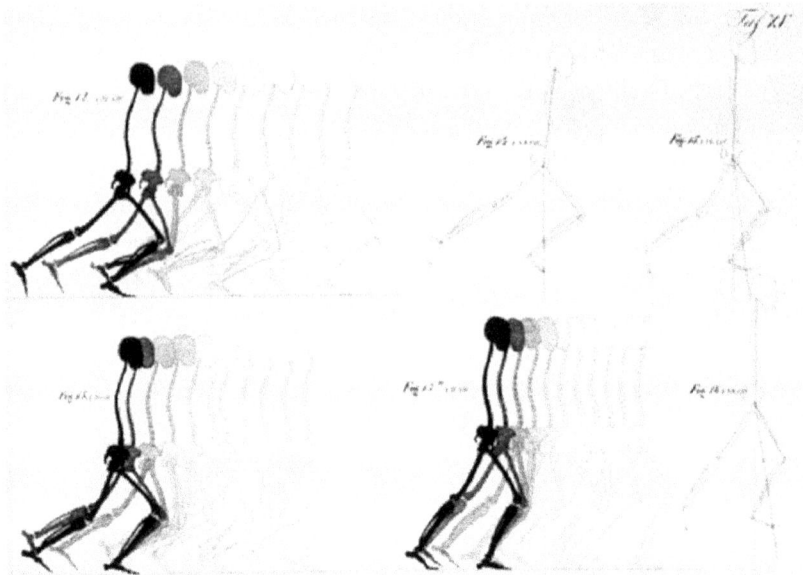

Figure 2 Wilhelm and Eduard Weber, *Mechanik der menschlichen Gehwerkzeuge*, plate 15 (1836).

Physiology of Walking': 'It is a most complex, violent and perilous operation, which we divest of its extreme danger only by continual practice from a very early period of life' (Holmes, 1883, 127). Arthur Schopenhauer described walking in *The World as Will and Representation* as 'a continuously checked falling' (Schopenhauer, 2010, 337–8), to which the character named in Schopenhauer's honour alludes in *Watt*: Arthur 'watched his legs as under him they moved, in and out. I stand first on one leg, he said, then on the other, so, and in that way I move forward. Notice how without thinking you avoid the daisies, he said. What sensibility' (Beckett, 2009c, 221).

Even to Beckett's alienated characters the gait is an inalienable trait, a proof of personal identity that literally establishes minimum equilibrium. Their locomotion rather than their face is typically presented as the index to their character, and thus described with the close attention that Honoré de Balzac had urged in his 1833 *Théorie de la démarche*, which (revising Lavater) declares: 'La démarche est la physionomie du corps' (Balzac, 2016, 64) – walking is the physiognomy of the body. Evicted from home, the layabout of 'The Expelled' sets off, his step very much the physiognomy of his character, history and fate. 'Quelle allure' (Beckett, 1958b, 36):

> What a gait. Stiffness of the lower limbs, as if nature had denied me knees, extraordinary splaying of the feet to the right and left of the line of march. The trunk, on the contrary, as if by the effect of a compensatory mechanism, was as flabby as an old ragbag, tossing wildly to the unpredictable jolts of the

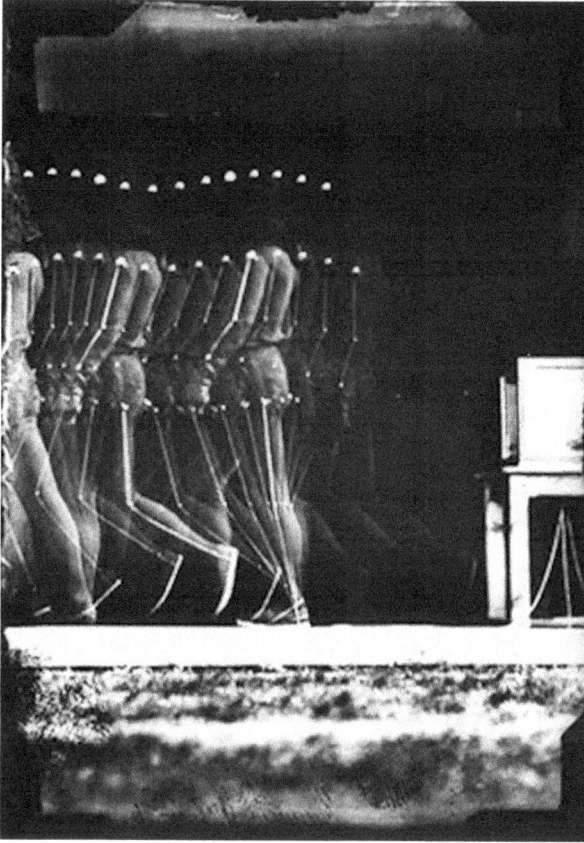

Figure 3 Étienne-Jules Marey, *Homme qui marche* (1891).

pelvis. I have often tried to correct these defects, to stiffen my bust, flex my knees and walk with my feet in front of one another, for I had at least five or six, but it always ended the same way, I mean with a loss of equilibrium, followed by a fall. A man must walk without paying attention to what he's doing, as he sighs, and when I walked without paying attention to what I was doing I walked in the way I have just described, and when I began to pay attention I managed a few steps of creditable execution and then fell. I decided therefore to be myself. (Beckett, 1995, 50)

The expelled confirms the paradox that hobbles Zeno Cosini in Italo Svevo's novel *The Confessions of Zeno*, which Beckett's mentor James Joyce had been instrumental in publishing. Convulsed by a friend's explanation of 'the enormous complexity' of bipedal mechanics, Zeno can now scarcely keep from falling: 'I left that café limping and for several days always limped. Walking had become for me an onerous labour, and also slightly painful. That tangle of mechanisms seemed in need now of oil and in moving the parts damaged each other' (Svevo, 1987, 106; my translation).

In the psychoanalytic literature that their work explicitly engages, Svevo and Beckett could read how a walking disorder emerges as a process of symbolization. In *Studies in Hysteria*, Sigmund Freud and Josef Breuer ascribe Cäcelie v. M's disabling heel pain to a fear of being unable to find herself 'on a right footing' in society (Breuer and Freud, 1955, 179). In 'The Uncanny' Freud describes how a town saunter uncannily maps an otherwise unconscious involuntary compulsion (see Freud, 1970, 259–60). In *Beyond the Pleasure Principle* he conceives of psychoanalysis itself in pedestrian terms, quoting Rückert's aphorism *Was man nicht erfliegen kann, muß man erhinken*: what can't be flown to must be limped (Freud, 1959, 110). He literally wanted Cäcelie v. M to learn to limp into society rather than avoid it altogether. The expelled, who ascribes his irremediable gait to the primal scene of botched toilet training, and who walks in the street to avoid barging into pedestrians, rejects the etiquette that renders his walk precarious and instead embraces his deformity.

The gait in Beckett can be grotesque, as in the case of 'The Expelled' or *Watt*, but it is not a cartoonish device, or without peculiar dignity. It is the means by which one is fundamentally situated in the world, affirming an individual, transitory, vulnerable embodiment. Walking can be palliative (Belacqua's neurotic release in *More Pricks than Kicks*), an epistemic vehicle (the pursuit of art recorded in the 'German Diaries', Moran's pursuit in *Molloy*), a regression (Molloy's return to his mother, O's to his mother's hovel in *Film*), a repudiation of societal expectations (in the *nouvelles* and 'From an Abandoned Work'), or a mourning regimen (the widow of 'One Evening' and the widower of *Ohio Impromptu*), but it crucially comes to serve as an ontological warrant – morbidly in *Footfalls* and *All That Fall*, elegiacally in *Ill Seen Ill Said*, and irenically in *Worstward Ho*.

In a 27 February 1934 letter to Nuala Costello, Beckett extolled 'this delicious conception of movement as gress, pure and mere gress', defining it as 'purity from destination and hence from schedule' (Beckett, 2009b, 186). Gression, shorn of the purposive prepositional accretions by which it is alone familiar (pro-, re-, e-, in-, con-, ag-, di- and transgress), is here not ascetic renunciation of purpose but voluptuous flight from it. And is becoming a kind of rest. In a 6 February 1936 letter to Thomas MacGreevy, Beckett adapted an Italian aphorism he had already quoted to him five months earlier: 'Have been walking feverishly, with [brother] Frank & alone. *Quando il piede cammina, il cuore gode*. "Gode" is rather strong. "Posa" would be better' (Beckett, 2009b, 313). 'When the foot walks the heart cheers', or rather, for the man suffering then from an arrhythmic heart, 'rests'.[1] He continued: 'For hours last Sunday along the

---

[1] The qualification evokes Giacomo Leopardi's 'To Himself' ('A se stesso'): 'My tired heart' ('*Stanco mio cor*') should 'rest for ever' ('*Posa per sempre*') (Leopardi, 1998, 510, 512). Ailing Belacqua recites the passage in *Dream of Fair to Middling Women*: '*Or posa per sempre*, for

ridge between Glendalough & Glenmalure. And alone anything from 5 to 10 miles locally daily. It saves cafard & masturbation' (313). On a Sunday in the Wicklow hills to which his father and he had formerly fled from church services, Beckett found distraction from Belacqua's 'chinks' (*cafard*) and Murphy's libido. Later he found in it more than a mere hiatus.

Beckett wrote to Mary Manning on 13 December 1936 that his peripatetic German trip 'has turned out indeed to be a journey *from*, & not *to*, as I knew it was, before I began it' (Beckett, 2009b, 397). He would eventually transcend such directional coordinates, but not the extensive walking. Shortly after returning to Dublin from Germany, Beckett wrote to MacGreevy on 26 March 1937 that 'I like walking more & more, the less aim the better' (Beckett, 2009b, 489). At this time Beckett finds an enabling interdependence of flux and fixity; motiveless mobility secures a kind of camouflaged stasis. In the second entry in the *Whoroscope Notebook*, begun in 1935, Beckett conceives of a 'dynamist ethic' that would figure prominently in his work: 'Keep moving the only virtue' (UoR MS3000,1 r; qtd in Ackerley, 2012, 145).

Ultimately this intransitive walk goes from a mere fugue or subterfuge to a basic value, from which Beckett derives not only a distinctive narrative and dramatic structure but a governing trope for elusive being. The random walk becomes the instantiation of life directed not to determinate ends but along paths independent of motive and destination, reviving afoot an anti-teleological philosophical tradition in which Beckett immersed himself. Among extensive notes made from Arnold Geulincx' *Ethica* in 1936 at Trinity College Dublin, Beckett summed up the seventeenth century philosopher's quietist triad *abitus transitus aditus* – coming biding going: 'totus sum (totus hunc veniendo, totus hic agendo, totus hinc abeundo)' – 'I have my whole being (in coming hither, acting here, departing hence)' (TCD MS 10971/6/25 and Geulincx, 2006, 337; qtd in Tucker, 2012, 84). The single dimly emancipatory impulse in Beckett is errancy itself, life as meshwork of ways rather than network of stations; coming-biding-going as the ineradicable nucleus of human possibility and ethical meanings, as in the poem 'thither': 'thither ... then there ... then hence' (Beckett, 2012, 206). And in the roundelay from *Watt* that Beckett valued enough to record:

> Watt will not
> abate one jot
> but of what
> of the coming to

---

example, he was liable to murmur, lifting and shifting the seat of the disturbance, *stanco mio cor* ' (Beckett, 1993, 61–2). Leopardi's poem is quoted in *Proust* and furnishes its epigraph.

> of the being at
> of the going from
> knott's habitat
> of the long way
> of the short stay
> of the going back home
> the way he had come
> of the empty heart
> of the empty hands
> of the dim mind wayfaring (Beckett, 2009c, 218)

In contrast to Christian and Enlightenment progress, gress is not remedial or soteriological but ontological, an amble on to being. However impeded his specific characters may be, being in Beckett inheres in bipedalism. A categorical human propensity becomes a dispositional one as well, the determinate quality commensurate with what the human does: slowly walk vast distances however inhospitable. Experience reduces to and depends on being a 'poor, bare, forked animal', and understanding arises from this fact, as wandering unaccommodated Lear realises (King Lear III, iv, 110, Shakespeare, 1959, 122). And, as being defies definition, Beckett's conspicuous tropes of walking enact impaired approach to it. The aimless walk epitomises the 'integrity of incoherence' that Beckett sought to preserve in his work as the ineradicable condition of being (qtd in O'Reilly, Van Hulle and Verhulst, 2017, 377).

Whereto next, Vladimir asks Pozzo, who replies: 'Je ne m'occupe pas de ça' (Beckett, 1971, 129). In translation however Beckett hit upon the kernel: 'On' (Beckett, 1982b, 102). The preposition obtains the mass of a noun and the force of a verb, and then, as in *Embers*, surpasses both to become a morphemic cipher of transitive and elusive being, or *on*tology. Being, that is, glimpsed only in passing, and so perpetually deferred: on towards being, be it towards some final constitution, restitution or confrontation. This *on*tology may be as much a procedure as a performance, a method in at least the etymological sense (*met' hodos*): steps 'along the way' to being. When translating *L'Innommable*, which originally ended 'je ne peux pas continuer' without the epigrammatic disclaimer, Beckett borrowed from Pozzo's pith: 'I can't go on, I will go on' (Beckett, 1958a, 179). Only from the novel's second edition does the French add 'je vais continuer' (Beckett, 1953, 213). That reiteration is a brash variation on ploce or conduplicatio – a rhetorical repetition modifying the sense. The first 'go on' is an admission, the sequel a resolution; the first is an existential negation, the second an ontological affirmation.

They typically 'go on' foot in Beckett. W. G. Sebald, who pays homage to him in *Unrecounted*, suggested in an interview that 'there can be something like a physiology of literature, that is, that our embodiment and the way we move our body can be transferred to literature' (Sebald, 2012, 251; my translation). In this literary physiology (including Sebald's *The Rings of Saturn*) themes are scavenged along paths and cognition is participatory and distributed across the peripatetic body. Beckett's meandering texts often have a fortuitous and circumstantial organization predicated on homologies between walking, thinking and narration implicit in the etymological 'wayward step' of digression. In the first English manual of style, the 1589 *Arte of English Poesie*, George Puttenham calls digression the 'straggler', personifying as a pedestrian the figure of verbal deviation (Puttenham, 2007, 318). Digressive speech matches digressive gait.

Desultory stroll becomes desultory text, steps functioning as signifiers constituting a subtext or subliminal language. As Merlin Coverley observes in *The Art of Wandering*, 'Aimlessness leads to the aim while firm intentions often miss' (Coverley, 2012, 163). From a Lacanian perspective, this accords with the very structure of the unconscious and thus, for Slavoj Žižek, the essence of psychoanalysis: realizing what can be grasped only obliquely and without aim. As the Beckett walk becomes more random, it however sheds the accompanying psychic content that might elucidate and justify the walking cure. In *The Unnamable*, Beckett writes: 'A desirable goal, no, I never had time to dwell on that. To go on, I still call that on, to go on and get on has been my only care, if not always in a straight line, at least in obedience to the figure assigned to me' (Beckett, 1958a, 45). Psyche cedes to footsole. By eschewing ends the Beckett walk deters instrumental calculation long enough to approach a goal, be it plenum or vacuum, that can only be neared without itinerary.

Beckett's pedestrian poetics has entered the work of many artists, not least Sebald's meandering excurses, Iain Sinclair's stalking of Beckett's London in *London Overground*, and Bruce Nauman's performance piece *Slow Angle Walk (Beckett Walk)*. The itineracy in Harold Pinter's play *The Caretaker*, the wasteland trudge of father and son in Cormac McCarthy's novel *The Road*, the metaphysical sleuthing of Paul Auster's novel *City of Glass*, the ambulatory automatism of Joshua Ferris's novel *The Unnamed*, the desert fugue of Wim Wenders' film *Paris, Texas*, and the homage walk of Anne Carson's poem 'Quad' follow directly in Beckett's footprints. While much art has been inspired by pedestrianism in his work, scholarship has not given it close attention. Yet, as mobility studies and direct pedestrian activism flourish, especially in the wake of public health measures restricting movement during the pandemic, the Beckett walk has never had as much to say.

Romantic Vagrancy

Walking is semiotic as well as mechanical, belonging to social as well as physical mobility. The Beckett walk oscillates between species universal and individually imprinted social norm, for it is at once a primal activity, a cultural practice and a distinctive personal trait. Enlightenment kinesiological attempts to define human locomotion foundered in part on the cultural and idiosyncratic variety of gait, which had fascinated and vexed Balzac in *Théorie de la démarche* (see Mayer, 2020, 142). The Beckett walk comes out of the Laetoli tuff that preserved the earliest imprint of the hominins 3.6 million years ago, out of Victorian standards of comportment, and not least out of literature. As Anne D. Wallace cautions in *Walking, Literature and English Culture*, 'to see walking as text and text as walking by its rambling narrative structures and examples of pedestrian composition without acknowledging literature's representations of walking' is an historical falsification (Wallace, 1993, 194). Literary, artistic, stage and musical representations prepare the Beckett walk, so the first step is to situate it in the Edwardian, Victorian and Romantic contexts that largely determined it.

Jeffrey Robinson states that 'the walk is a quintessentially Romantic image', a preferred trope of inwardness, liberty, nonconformity, withdrawal and inspiration

Figure 4 Caspar David Friedrich, *Northern Landscape, Spring* (c. 1825); Collection National Gallery, Washington.

(Robinson, 2006, 5). Beckett's ambivalent assimilation of Romanticism, disavowed but never relinquished, can be measured in footfalls, for such tropes proliferate throughout his work, even as walking is not for him, as for Rousseau, Wordsworth and Hölderlin, a means of self-cultivation, self-disclosure, social levelling, or nature piety (*Naturfrömmigkeit*). With reference to Caspar David Friedrich's *Two Men Observing the Moon* (an acknowledged inspiration for *Waiting for Godot*), Beckett in a 14 January 1937 German diary entry extols a *bémolisé* or minor key Romanticism – inward, unappeased, disenchanted, antirational, pessimistic and sublunary (see Figure 4): 'pleasant predilection for 2 tiny languid men in his landscapes, as in the little moon landscape, that is the only kind of romantic still tolerable, the bémolisé' (Beckett qtd in Nixon, 2011, 142).

From the early poems 'Dieppe' and 'The Vulture' (inspired by walking poems of Hölderlin and Goethe) to the stravager issuing forth daily 'to walk the roads' from dawn to dusk in the late teleplay ... *but the clouds* ... (Beckett, 1984, 259), Beckett's solitary walkers are the outcome of an indelible Romantic type, including Rousseau's *promeneur solitaire*, Wordsworth's vagrants, the wanderers of Friedrich's landscapes, the outcast of the Schubert/Müller *Winterreise* and the *peregrini* of Leopardi. In the mid-1930s he transcribed into a notebook lines from Goethe's *Faust*: 'Im Weiterschreiten find' er Qual und Glück,/ Er! Unbefriedigt jeden Augenblick' (Beckett, TCD MS10971/1, 35 r; see Nixon, 2011, 73; *Faust*, ll. 11451–2; Goethe, 1986, 345) – 'In striding on he finds torment and happiness,/ he! discontented every moment!'

On the precedent of Rousseau and Wordsworth, the walk in Beckett is a textual figure, a framing device and a material practice. His desublimated reimagining of the Romantic pedestrian archetype, shorn of revolutionary-era metaphysical and political idealism, moral uplift, or veneration of nature, proceeds from a regressive narcissism and transgressive automatism to a congressive quietism. The *via negativa* becomes a shared path of disavowed agency and apophatic ignorance. These dispositions are not strictly chronological but recursive, like many a Beckett walk, and represent the partial rehabilitation of Romanticism that is one hallmark of waning Modernism.

Romanticism made of the idle promenade an individuating affirmation of the inviolable integrity of the mind – the idealism of the Jena coterie stepping out in tramping garb.[2] In *Les Rêveries du promeneur solitaire*, one of several of

---

[2] 'Die erste Idee ist natürlich die Vorstellung *von mir Selbst*, als einem absolut freien Wesen. Mit dem freien, selbstbewußten Wesen tritt zugleich eine ganze *Welt* – aus dem Nichts hervor' [The first idea is naturally the representation *of my self*, as an absolute free entity. Together with the free, self-assured entity steps forth an entire *world*] (Hölderlin, 1963, 556). My translation preserves the pedestrial basis of the verb of emergence *hervortreten*. *The Unnamable* is the zenith and nadir of this neo-Kantian idealism.

Rousseau's works cited in Beckett's *Dream* notebook and early letters, walking conditions perception by making explicit the body's participation in cognition. Thought, writing and bipedal movement calibrate. In a book organised into casual *promenades* without theme, narrative or purpose, *le discours* cedes to *le parcours*: informal and spontaneous, the promenades follow 'their bent without resistance and without interference' ('*leur pente sans résistance et sans gêne*') (Rousseau, 1997, 64) in a discontinuous ('*peu de liaison*'; 61) and unsystematic ('*sans réduire en systeme*'; 62) succession. Anxieties and wearying reflection ebb with the dissolution of the ego into the immensity of nature and thus into an embrace of mortality. The book gave Beckett a precedent for what O'Reilly, Van Hulle and Verhulst call an *écriture à processus*, an unprogrammatic principle of spontaneous composition that culminated in the trilogy of novels and *Texts for Nothing* (O'Reilly, Van Hulle and Verhulst, 2017, 153; see also Van Hulle and Verhulst, 2017a, 29). To MacGreevy he wrote on 16 September 1934: 'But always the background of the promeneur solitaire, micturating without fear or favour in a décor that does not demand to be entertained' (Beckett, 2009b, 228).

Walking recovers the self in safeguarded anonymity, not only a replenishing evasion of society but of its internalised imperatives, as when Henry David Thoreau notes in 'Walking' that it is an hour into the woods before Concord is truly behind him. For arch-denouncer of society Rousseau, the walk fosters constancy to the sole self he calls *amour de soi*, the dispassionate sentiment of existence, free of all belittling proprietary entanglements (*amour propre*). Beckett hails Rousseau as an 'authentically tragic figure' in his 16 September 1934 letter to MacGreevy: a heroic 'champion of the right to be alone' in a world that viewed 'solitude as a vice' (Beckett, 2009b, 227). Yet for Beckett the philosopher is lured into libidinal snares. Sexual dependence is depicted in a Romantic vein already in his first published story, 'Assumption', then sardonically debunked in *More Pricks than Kicks, Murphy* and 'First Love'. The quest for autarky leads Belacqua and Murphy to an unsustainable solipsism. The latter character, Chris Ackerley notes, 'is an image of peripatetic motion, the monad as nomad' (Ackerley, 2012, 149). Later the alterity of language and ultimately of the very self renders specious the seclusion of the *promeneur solitaire*, yet Beckett never altogether sloughs the pathos of unattainable Rousseauvian autonomy. In ... *but the clouds* ... the compulsive stravager returns nightly to his dim 'sanctum' to resume his Romantic necrophilia, imploring the beautiful apparition who, intermittently appearing in chiaroscuro close-up, mouths the stanza from W. B. Yeats' 'The Tower' that gives the 1977 teleplay its title (Beckett, 1984, 259).

The ascendency of the autonomous Kantian mind that Romanticism equated with walking, as in Friedrich Schiller's ode "The Walk ('Der Spaziergang') and William Hazlitt's essay 'On Going a Journey', which culminated on the Mount

Snowdon of Wordsworth's *The Prelude*, already began to founder for the latter's fell-walking companion Coleridge, whose identification of nature with mind could not resolve estranging dualism. Though rural settings rather than metropoles dominate his work, Beckett denigrates the equation in an 8 September 1934 letter to MacGreevy: 'after all the landscape "promoted" to the emotions of the hiker, postulated as *concerned* with the hiker (what an impertinence, worse than Aesop and the animals), alive the way a lap or a *fist* (Rosa) is alive. Cézanne seems to be the first to see landscape & state it as material of a strictly peculiar order, incommensurable with all human expressions whatsoever' (Beckett, 2009b, 222). Where the egotistical sublime of Wordsworth and Rousseau identifies itself with nature in order finally to transmute it into providential hieroglyphs of the mind's ascendency over matter, Beckett does not substitute nature piety for the religious variety.

Beckett belongs to the post-Romantic deflation: disappointed is the reconciliation of social and religious contraries through peripatetic immersion in a moralised nature of universal analogy. Failed projector of internal states, nature is no longer means to the renewal of the 'shaping spirit of Imagination' wanting in Coleridge's 'Dejection: An Ode' (Coleridge, 1951, 80). Instead proliferate pedestrian tropes of separation and self-estrangement in vacant regions that foment solipsistic self-consciousness – in other words, a Romantic agony. In the terse 1934 elegy 'Echo's Bones', Beckett links mourning his father to walking and a death-wish: 'asylum under my tread all this day' (Beckett, 2012, 23). The crone of 'Enough' and other works bend into the walking posture of Wordsworth's old Cumberland beggar:

> One little span of earth
> Is all his prospect. Thus from day to day
> Bow-bent, his eyes forever on the ground,
> He plies his weary journey; [. . . .]
> His staff trails with him; scarcely do his feet
> Disturb the summer dust (Wordsworth, 1954, 116).

The widow beyond the cabin of *Ill Seen Ill Said* is 'riveted to some detail of the desert' ('L'oeil fixant sur un détail du désert'; Beckett, 1996, 56; 1981, 21): the veiled figments who withdraw while 'her footprints are effaced' in the snow ('la trace de ses pas s'efface'; 1996, 55; 1981, 19). Beckett recasts Coleridge's lament for the shaping spirit of the imagination: 'Imagination at wit's end spreads its sad wings' (1996, 56).[3] A contracted *Winterreise* rises, in Beckett's self-translation, to

---

[3] Altering the original, where the 'madwoman' gives in to her tears: 'La folle du logis s'en donne à coeur chagrin' (Beckett, 1981, 21).

the alliterative trochaic pentameter of Sir Gawain's winter journey to the Green Knight: 'Winter in her winter haunts she wanders' (55).[4]

'Je vais déjeuner', Beckett wrote to Georges Duthuit from Foxrock on 27 July 1948 of his summer haunts, 'puis aller me promener sur les longues pentes vertes d'où enfant je voyais par temps clair les montagnes du Pays de Galles. À la nuit tombante mon père, pour m'amuser, mettait feu au genêt' ['I am going to have lunch then go for a walk on the long green slopes from where, on a clear day, when I was a child, I used to see the mountains of Wales. As night fell my father, to amuse me, used to set fire to the broom'] (Beckett, 2011, 84, 87). Sentimental treks to verdant hillsides where his father once showed him vistas across the sea and lit him bonfires at sunset: to suppress such *féerique* overtones of Celtic picturesque for a Paris correspondent he adds, 'Paysage romantique mais promeneur bien sec' ['Romantic landscape, but dry old stick of a traveler'] (84, 87).

The Romantic wayfarer bore all too visibly for Beckett the ideological overtone of insurgent Irish nationalism: the dispossession of pariah, saint, insurgent, refugee, fugitive, migrant labourer. Yet, shorn of existential uplift, national feeling and natural religion, the Beckett misfit aspires to the resolution and independence of the old Cumberland beggar and the leech-gatherer. The formula of a checked but not repudiated Romanticism Beckett will often reprise. The *promeneur bien sec* of 'From an Abandoned Work' sardonically reiterates *Childe Harold's Pilgrimage*: blaspheming disaffection, torpid detachment, anhedonia, aboulia, disgust and yearning for oblivion: 'Up bright and early that day, I was young then, feeling awful, and out' (Beckett, 1995, 155). The melancholic's cursed excursions return him unredeemed to the suffocating family seat shared with his widowed mother, but he does not crave scope or variety. Rather he is always 'stravaging the same old roads in all weathers, I was never much of a one for new ground' (158). Beckett's fatherless Childe does not traverse battlefields, Rhine canyons, or toppled Roman masonry to arrive at *contemptus mundi*. Maledictions are not expressions of Romantic despair but of Turrets syndrome (see 163). He does not emulate Harold's homages to precursors or forsaken love. To 'the nympholepsy of some fond despair' (Byron, 1967, 149) he is inured: 'Never loved anyone I think, I'd remember' (Beckett, 1995, 158). His meditations on decay are closer even to Manfred's Weltschmerz than to Harold's: 'Over, over, there is a soft place in my heart for all that is over, no, for the being over, I love the word, words have been my only loves, not many' (162).

This anemically recalls Harold's yearning to distil language 'into one word': 'And that one word were lightning, I would speak' (Byron, 1967, 103–4). That

---

[4] 'Hiver elle erre chez elle l'hiver' (Beckett, 1981, 18).

one word, discharging not light but dimness, will again be *on*: 'But let me get on now with the day I have hit on to begin with, any other would have done as well, yes, on with it and out of my way and on to another' (Beckett, 1995, 156). The repeated idiom *going on* strikes the homology between walking and writing, as when Beckett adds a pun on *none*: 'what is the sense of going on with all this, there is none' (162). Self-disgust soon discontinues the relation. Yet abandoning a work only to then publish the fragment recalls Coleridge heeding Byron's advice to publish 'Kubla Khan'. From an abandoned work to the consummately Romantic fragment is but a step.

Beyond a great 'love in my heart for all things still and rooted', Byronic absorption in nature cannot be maintained (Beckett, 1995, 155). Beckett's narrator is pursued by stoats, takes a fall and sinks into a thicket of giant ferns. Walking is an abject compulsion rather than a panacea: 'vent the pent, that was one of those things I used to say, over and over, as I went along, vent the pent, vent the pent' (158). His ubiquitous ashplant is cutlass as well as crutch: 'My stick of course, by a merciful providence. I shall not say this again, when not mentioned my stick is in my hand, as I go along' (161). This walking stick becomes the vehement libidinal proxy that Wordsworth brandishes in 'Nutting': 'the next thing I was up in the bracken lashing about with my stick making the drops fly and cursing, filthy language, the same words over and over' (163) – beloved word *over*. Like his expletives, the wanton strokes are involuntary profanations: 'the lashing about with the stick, what possessed me mild and weak to be doing that' (163). After Wordsworth's 'merciless ravage' with his nutting-crook comes shame, remorse and rehabilitating pantheism, 'for there is a spirit in the woods' (Wordsworth, 1952, 212); in Beckett by contrast comes squalor, derangement and menace, where not waving daffodils but serrated ferns abound: 'break your leg if you're not careful, awful English this, fall and vanish from view, you could lie there for weeks and no one hear you' (Beckett, 1995, 164).

In the first panegyric to pedestrianism, 'On Going a Journey', William Hazlitt declares: 'When I am in the country, I wish to vegetate like the country' (Hazlitt, 1970, 136). He prefers solitude to society and a volume of Rousseau to conversation. 'The mind then is "its own place", nor are we anxious to arrive at the end of our journey', Hazlitt writes, quoting Milton's Satan like a Byronic renegade (145). The prospect onto the Dee valley 'opened to my inward sight, a heavenly vision, on which were written, in letters large as Hope could make them these four words, LIBERTY, GENIUS, LOVE, VIRTUE; which have since faded into the light of common day, or mock my idle gaze' (143). What mocks it is the *promeneur bien sec* Childe Harold, who above Athens perceives that veneration is transient and vain. Beckett's walkers do not indulge in it.

Beckett's meandering narrative vaguens a structure derived, like *Molloy*, from the internalised quest romance of the Romantic ode, which like *Childe Harold's Pilgrimage* Beckett then ruptures: outward into a seemingly change-less rural landscape that coaxes a vexed inwardness ('the rages were the worst, like a great wind suddenly rising in me'; Beckett, 1995, 157), eventually able to bestride the flux, then outward again and replenished towards home. This walk condenses a Romantic *Bildungsreise*, in M. H. Abrams' terms a formational journey from childhood's natural unity through maturation in mental and social division towards a renewed wholeness of *Naturfrömmigkeit* (see Abrams, 1971, 453–4). Like Schiller's 'The Walk', his solitary stravager hikes from town house 'up in the mountains' (Beckett, 1995, 164), seeking relief from repressive custom and social obligation, meditating on alienation and transience until overtaken by august natural emblems of reconciliation and transcendence. In Schiller's ode the chief of these is an eagle; in Beckett's fragment it is a radiant '*Schimmel*', 'the only completely white horse I remember' (157), which con-jures Theodore Sturm's post-Romantic tale *Der Schimmelreiter*.

Absent from Beckett are the analogies between nature, intellect and morality that Schiller extols, or that Coleridge intuits fell-walking above Cumberland: personal acedia overcome and philosophical dualism reconciled into Wordsworthian 'feel-ing intellect' to 'make nature thought, and thought nature' (Wordsworth, 1971, 522; Abrams, 1970, 222). In a notebook entry anticipating the metaphysical defence of the 'esemplastic' imagination in the *Biographia Literaria*, Coleridge writes: "This I call *I*, identifying the percipient and the perceived' (Coleridge qtd in Frye, 1963, 15; see Coleridge, 1907, 107). Even where he appears to stage such an identification, at the climax of *Film* when observer and observed fuse, it creates an ideogram of demonic inwardness, nearer to the Coleridge of 'Christabel' and *The Wanderings of Cain*. Again in a dialectical relation to Romanticism, Beckett, following Leopardi, Byron and Hazlitt, forecloses re-integration. Drained of polit-ical content, the walk is anodyne rather than uplifting. In this internalised quest romance the self is not harmonised, and like Childe Harold, or the wanderer (*peregrino*) scaling Vesuvius in Leopardi's excursive ode 'Broom' ('La Ginestra') (Leopardi, 1998, 614), he achieves imaginative freedom at the cost of morose self-consciousness and social separation (see Bloom, 1970, 5–16).

This is less a refutation of Romanticism than the Romantic agony of Mario Praz's book, which Beckett read shortly after publication in 1930. The strava-ger's dilatory reflections are paced out in Beckett's 'From an Abandoned Work':

> from the dim granted ground to its things and the sky the eyes raised and
> back again, raised again and back again again, and the feet going nowhere
> only somehow home, in the morning out from home and in the evening back

home again, and the sound of my voice all day long muttering the same old things I don't listen to, not even mine it was at the end of the day … (Beckett, 1995, 159)

This is no Helm Crag paced while inditing a *Prelude*, only self-alienated logorrhea. Although Beckett's vagrants, like those of an Irish Romanticism responding to Catholic dispossession and the Famine, owe something to Wordsworth's, they are remote from the 'consummate happiness' and 'restoration' from 'unacknowledged weariness' of 'Resolution and Independence' (Wordsworth, 1952, 240).

'I have never in my life been on my way anywhere, but simply on my way' (Beckett, 1995, 156). The walks conjured in 'From an Abandoned Work' have neither distinction nor destination. The fragment breaks at self-estranged onwardness: he 'just went on, my body doing its best without me' (164). There is no restitution of inner to outer, only anticipation of when 'it will not be as now, day after day, out, on, round, back, in', but instead gressive, 'a long unbroken time without before or after, light or dark, from or towards or at' (163). While the story's title may invite psychoanalytical interpretation in light of Beckett's abandoned treatment under Wilfred Bion at the Tavistock clinic twenty years earlier, the narrator's compulsive, unmotivated treks beyond his mother's house are notable for voiding psychic content. He is walking out on diagnostics. The talking cure is reduced to a sore throat from spouting nonsense even he no longer hears. Therapeutic goals could only be happened upon aimlessly.

Victorian and Edwardian Tramping

The Romantics' withdrawal into inner worlds, their preference for expressivist over mimetic representation, and predilection for fragmentary oneiric states and dusky deserted natural settings permanently inflected Beckett's imagination, along with a dynamic model of being that drew them to the walk. Journey becomes place in Beckett's work, denuded of the landscape paraphernalia that filled the Claude glass of Romanticism since William Gilpin's popularization of the picturesque. Sublime scenery, exotic regional customs, edifying local encounters and parish landmarks leave no impression; Beckett's postwar fiction will not satisfy a continental appetite for misty vistas of Celtic moor and gorse. The hard pastoral of the Irish Revival and the soft georgics of the Georgian anthologies were antiquarian obfuscations. Neither oaten reed nor easel *en plein air* for Beckett's art, which travels light. The walk is anoetic rather than meditative. *How It Is*, *Quad* and 'The Way' repudiate the rectory moralizing of T. S. Eliot's 'Little Gidding'; the end of our journey deposits us where we started but unappeased by knowledge – beyond knowledge, rather.

That the *promeneur solitaire bien sec* might stalk out of Romantic sensibility by Romantic paths Beckett could see in the art of Jack B. Yeats, several of whose landscapes Beckett acquired and whose work he promoted (see Figure 8). Yeats's walkers in a minor key escape nationalist iconography, natural supernaturalism, and existential uplift. The vagrant from 'Walking Out' steps out of a Yeats canvas, as does the singing wagoner across the still moor evoked by innkeeper Gast in *Mercier and Camier* (Beckett, 1988, 52–3; 1970a, 81–2). In Yeats's landscapes the walker modulates from scruffy subject to human staffage measuring the disproportionate scale of the mineral earth. Pim crawling in the mud is a Leopardi-inflected ('*e fango è il mondo*' – Krapp's 'old muckball'; Beckett, 1984, 62) extension of Jack Yeats' man merging with fuchsia hedge and path as rain-clouds gather in *A Storm*, a painting Beckett admired in a 14 August 1937 letter to Thomas MacGreevy (Beckett, 2009b, 540).

The social and ideological re-definition of walking in the aftermath of Rousseau (see Jarvis, 1997, 4 and 62) was still palpable in the Britain and Ireland of Beckett's youth, where the unpurposive walk could discreetly manifest cultural nostalgia and genteel dissent from the positivist, utilitarian, mechanistic, capitalist habitus of empire. The Coleridgian zeal to overcome dualism and harmonise body, mind and world, in particular after the posthumous 1850 publication of the epic addressed to Coleridge, Wordsworth's *The Prelude*, promoted the Victorian and Edwardian vogue for countryside hiking that the transport revolution facilitated. An increasingly sedentary middle class in the polluted metropolis made walking a health fad, like those ridiculed in Lucky's tirade and *Act without Words II*. Then as now, the potential benefits of walking were treated as inherent properties. Leisurely tramping was a frugal, healthy exercise of personal autonomy and social levelling as against the privileges and demands of social caste. In sectarian Ireland, the ramble additionally provided a Protestant alternative to Catholic pilgrimage, such as that on Station Island in County Donegal, denounced in the early nineteenth century by the apostate William Carleton in 'The Lough Derg Pilgrim'.

Thoreau placed walkers in an alternative peerage in 'Walking': 'The chivalric and heroic spirit which once belonged to the Rider seems now to reside in, or perchance to have subsided into, the Walker – not the Knight, but Walker, Errant. He is a sort of fourth estate, outside of Church and State and People' (Thoreau, 1980, 94). Walt Whitman, whom Thoreau met and praised in his journal, invoked not the walker but the open road, an actant imparting secret truths and trespass: 'the universe itself as a road, as many roads, as roads for traveling souls' (Whitman, 1996, 187). Whitman's acolyte, the naturalist John Burroughs praised in 'The Exhilaration of the Road' the British right of access legislation that facilitated the walks of Beckett's father, and he celebrated the pedestrian virtues of pragmatic, frank, modest mobility that William Beckett embodied for the son he invited on his hikes. In walking, 'man returned to first principles' and achieved a 'state of grace' (Burroughs, 1896, 37 and 40), Burroughs claimed, an emphasis relevant to Beckett's father, who turned to the hills while his pious wife filed towards Sunday church service. 'He was sighing for the golden age; let him walk to it. Every step brings him nearer. The youth of the world is but a few days' journey distant' (48). In the spirit of Whitman's open road, Burroughs praises 'that happy, delicious, excursive vagabond' (52), who experiences the 'magnetic touch' of soles: 'Man takes root at his feet' (54). He admires the tramp's barefoot triumph over a degenerate society constrained by thick-soles and high-heels: the foot is 'sensuous and alive', an 'athlete among consumptives' (52). The walker 'is not merely a spectator of the panorama of nature, but a participator in it', able to read 'the mute language of things' (47).

Like Burroughs a naturalist, W. H. Hudson finds respite rather than liberation while *Afoot in England*: from caste in a farmer's kitchen, from motorcars on Salisbury Plain after midnight, from seaside tourist resorts, from purposiveness altogether. The reprieve will not forestall the advance of industrial agronomy, mechanised transport and the hospitality industry. Hudson's celebration of a 'gorgeous' tramp, 'handsome' and 'irreclaimable' in fashionable cast-offs, resembles Belacqua's admiration for the tramp in 'Walking Out'. Unlike Beckett, Hudson does not discount the pauper's physical and moral privations as they pick late blackberries (Hudson, 1982, 115), but he anticipates Beckett's aimless landlopers who expect not deliverance but simple palliation.

Unlike his earlier *Travels with a Donkey*, R. L. Stevenson's panegyric 'Walking Tours' made the practice safe from antinomian innuendo and aesthetic decadence: 'He who is indeed of the brotherhood does not voyage in quest of the picturesque, but of certain jolly humours – of the hope and spirit with which the march begins at morning, and the peace and spiritual repletion of the evening's rest' (Stevenson, 1946, 139). In quoting from it he celebrates Hazlitt's essay but filters out the political idealism: 'Give me the clear blue sky over my head, and the green turf beneath my feet, a winding road before me, and a three hours' march to dinner – and then to thinking! It is hard if I cannot start some game on these lone heaths. I laugh, I run, I leap, I sing for joy' (142, quoting Hazlitt, 1970, 137). This was the almost innocent promise of walking when young Beckett accompanied his father's walks, but already then he was learning the nonconformism latent in this seemingly innocuous pastime.

The regular Sunday Tramps, organised primarily in Surrey by Leslie Stephens when 'Walking Tours' was published in 1881, added a soupçon of defiance to

Figure 5 *The Club-room on Zermatt in 1864,* from Edward Whymper,
Scrambles amongst the Alps (6th ed., London: John Murray, 1936, 218). Leslie
Stephen is seated left.

social respectability, anticipating the deviance of Beckett's socially descending
stravagers. The group advertised its agnosticism by sometimes hiking past
churches and chapels, and trespassed private reserves to assert pedestrian right of
access (though the members did not thereby risk prosecution for what was a mere
tort). In the 1902 encomium 'In Praise of Walking', the practice is recreation in
both senses, leisure and self-making, which put it in opposition to religious
orthodoxy. Vagrancy by now had been transformed from contravention to liberation (see e.g. Coverley, 2012, 69–70), if only for male gentility. Instead of the
ostentation and gourmandizing of venery and other aristocratic rural pursuits, the
thrifty hiker engaged in plain invigorating exertion; a contrast developed by
Stephen's comrade George Meredith in *The Egoist*, who fictionalised Virginia
Woolf's father as the lean otherworldly Alpinist Vernon Whitford, 'a man of quick
pace, the sovereign remedy for the dispersing of the mental fen-mist. He had tried it
and knew that nonsense was to be walked off' (Meredith, 1968, 157). Meredith was
an important precursor for Beckett's early style, but, along with his disillusioned
sonnet sequence *Modern Love*, Meredith's characterisation was also an influence,
and Vernon contributed to the character of Belacqua his reticence, evasiveness,
sexual ambivalence, and hapless need for personal sovereignty – all of which for
both unite in pedestrianism.[5] For the melancholy affliction of the 'chinks',

---

[5] In the wake of unwelcome sexual intercourse with the forward Smeraldina Rima, Belacqua in
Dream of Fair to Middling Women takes refuge in Meredith: 'his time of the lilies shifted over to

Belacqua's practice is 'to walk it off' (Beckett, 1974, 97) – what Vernon, borrowing from *King Lear*, calls 'my flibbertigibbet' (Meredith, 1968, 157). He does not simply walk off gloom or temper but, like fellow bachelor Belacqua, walks off from women: he 'walks away from the sex, not excelling in the recreations where men and women join hands' (111). This evasion, however, only makes him more alluring, and the humble and awkward pedestrian Whitford ultimately finds himself surpassing the suave horseman squire Sir Willoughby in the affection of the latter's disaffected fiancée Clara.

The deviation from social norms appears even in a respectable entrepreneur like Beckett's father William. As the Sunday trampers whistled past Mass, so he impiously failed to accompany the family to Sunday service at Tullow Church, despite his wife May's devoutness: 'Instead, he used to say "that he'd go to church with the birds up the mountains" and take himself off into the Dublin hills, alone or with one of his many friends. Later on, Beckett used to accompany him on these Sunday morning walks' (Knowlson, 1996, 42). Cousin Sheila Page, who summered at the Beckett house, Cooldrinagh, recalled that father and son 'went for wonderful walks. They were absolutely tuned in' (32). Hardship, exposure and masculine fellowship made tramping a choice field of middle-class male self-fashioning, into which William Beckett initiated his younger son, who also resented church attendance.

Hilaire Belloc, whose *The Old Road* and bestseller *The Path to Rome* had given fresh impetus to the literature of walking, argued in 'The Idea of a Pilgrimage' that 'the best way of all' to efface social division 'is on foot, where one is a man like any other man, with the sky above one, and the road beneath, and the world on every side, and time to see all' (Belloc, 1906, 234). Though a fervent Catholic, he generalises pilgrimage into wandering: 'For a man that goes on a pilgrimage does best of all if he starts out [. . .] with the heart of a wanderer, eager for the world as it is, forgetful of maps and descriptions, but hungry for real colours and men and the seeming of things' (235). This is the church with birds up in the mountains where William Beckett made his walks with his son.

Equally, however, the father's pedestrianism gauges the shift from gadabout to commuter. Urban growth and congestion stimulated fantasies of an untrammelled hinterland, increasingly accessible through transport infrastructure. Yet most of Ireland was in private and Crown possession that restricted access. 'Here? On my

---

the night hours, sitting vigilant among the rats, *alla fioca lucerna leggendo Meredith*' (Beckett, 1993, 18). Beckett modifies Leopardi's poem "Le ricordanze': '*Alla fioca lucerna poetando*" (Leopardi, 1998, 425). Belacqua 'is reading by the faint light' where the poet is 'inditing' (*poetando*).

land?' Pozzo confronts the apparent trespassers Vladimir and Estragon, grudging the public thoroughfare:

> Vladimir: We didn't intend any harm.
> Estragon: We meant well.
> Pozzo: The road is free to all.
> Vladimir: That's how we looked at it.
> Pozzo: It's a disgrace. But there you are. (Beckett, 1982b, 20)

The countryside, Joseph Amato writes, was reconceptualised for urbanites 'as a spiritual resource' (Amato, 2004, 202). William Beckett's construction of Cooldrinagh and his ambles in the rural environs paradoxically depended on just those transport technologies that would annex and degrade the local countryside. Railways and macadamised roads facilitated the capitalist property development of rural villages like Foxrock, ten miles from the city, into affluent suburbs that rendered remote countryside accessible to bourgeois recreation. Bid by Stevenson in *Travels with a Donkey in the Cévennes* to 'descend from the featherbed of civilization into the granite underfoot' (Stevenson, 2004, 35), William Beckett could depend on returning for a repast by nightfall.[6] Dan Rooney's commute in *All That Fall* repeats that of William Beckett from 6 Clare Street to Foxrock – and of his son from Trinity College. In the radio play (radio itself having an indispensable function in industrialised transport) the amenities are in transition: the train is not punctual, the still-unpaved road to the station is strewn with farm animals, the bicycle has a flat, the car is undependable, and no shuttle yet exists to convey the Rooneys from the station. The railway and carriageway are murderous defilements of a receding rural order, and the play accompanies a country woman's trudge rather than a city commuter's ride.[7]

Walking Cure

A native of the faux-georgic upscale suburb, Belacqua is a truant member of the class that elevated tramping to a leisure activity, shedding its associations with manual toil, social deviance and dispossession while exploiting its underclass allure. The Romantics, Robin Jarvis states, had made tramping 'a radical assertion of autonomy', an exercise in freedom from class expectations, education, upbringing

---

[6] Beckett told Knowlson that in earlier days his father would regularly take the train out to Rathfarnham to extend the walk home by ninety minutes (Knowlson, 1996, 32). Later he purchased increasingly luxurious automobiles, while his wife depended on a donkey-cart.

[7] Feargal Whelan notes that Beckett's imaginings of the Dublin commuter railway in *All That Fall* and *That Time* emphasise not the ease and efficiency of modern infrastructure but its limitations, malfunction and obsolescence (see Whelan, 2021). Yet the stalling, decrepit world of *All That Fall* is transmitted in an emerging electronic medium, and it is characteristic of Beckett to depict technology as vexatious but indomitable, and to find creative incentive in it.

and 'from a culturally defined and circumscribed self' (Jarvis, 1997, 28). In a narrow sense disdainful of moral uplift, aesthetic sublimity or political engagement, Belacqua aspires to this idealised footloose autonomy.

Like the narrators of the postwar *nouvelles*, Belacqua in *Dream of Fair to Middling Women* tries to best 'the bureaucratic mind' by walking away from it, but the privacy and ataraxy walking facilitates cannot be sustained because his solipsism, like Murphy's and Victor Krapp's later in *Eleutheria*, is comically far from impregnable (Beckett, 1993, 44). Walking dissipates the 'waking ultra-cerebral obscurity' he craves (44), in part because his 'ruined feet' and other pains are a constant reminder that the human body is imperfectly evolved for facultative bipedalism (8). The 'demolition of his feet' is the subject of clinical exposition:

> One: it was upon their outer rim that as a child, ashamed of his limbs that were ill-shaped, the knees that knocked, he walked. Boldly then he stepped off the little toe and the offside malleolus, hoping against hope to let a little light between the thighs, split the crural web and perhaps even who could tell, induce a touch of valgus elegance. Thereby alas he did but thicken the ankle, hoist the instep and detract in a degree that he does not care to consider from the male charm, and, who knows, the cogency, of the basin. (128)

Beyond Bloom's inspection of his toes in the 'Ithaca' episode of *Ulysses*, such virtuosic dilation on the lowly foot is almost unprecedented in realist fiction, a literary form that coincided with the industrialization of footwear. The Victorians recoiled from the foot's base contact with the soiling earth and endorsed its subjection to the executive functions of a lofty brain. The association with elemental sexuality that Belacqua insinuates in relating foot to pelvis had dictated displacement, as in the foot fetish for debutantes who dance more than walk in Alexander Pushkin's *Eugene Onegin*. Like the groin, the foot, conjoined in transgressive 'footsying' and lovers' walks, was to be clothed and demoted precisely because everywhere imposing an ineluctable fiat. Belacqua continues his exposition by turning to footwear: 'Two: as a youth, impatient of their bigness, contemptuous of the agonistic brogue, he shod them à la gigolo (a position he never occupied) in exiguous patents' (Beckett, 1993, 128). Rejecting Gaelic for continental footwear, he follows with the detailed, mordant history of pinching shoes purchased in Italy and in Germany, confirming the cherished adage of Thomas à Kempis's *Imitatio Christi*: 'the joyful going forth and sorrowful coming home' (129).[8] Relief never comes, so from Alba's flat at novel's end Belacqua limps still on 'his ruined feet' (237).

---

[8] In Paris Beckett attracted notoriety for wearing a yellow pair two sizes too small, handed down by Joyce. Van Hulle and Verhulst note that the shoes are bestowed on Malone (see Van Hulle and Verhulst, 2017a, 226–9 and 241; see also Van Hulle and Verhulst, 2017b, 233–4).

Yet in *More Pricks than Kicks* those feet are the sovereign remedy they were to Meredith's Vernon. Belacqua 'enlivened the last phase of his solipsism' in 'Ding-Dong' 'with the belief that the best thing he had to do was to move constantly from place to place' (Beckett, 1974, 35). He imagines, says the intradiegetic narrator ('We were Pylades and Orestes'; 36), that 'he could give what he called the Furies the slip by merely setting himself in motion' (35). In a book incorporating diction Beckett compiled in the *Dream* notebook from *The Anatomy of Melancholy*, Belacqua embarks on Robert Burton's walking cure: 'no better physic for a melancholy man than change of air, and variety of places, to travel abroad and see fashions [. . .]. For peregrination charms our senses with such unspeakable and sweet variety' (Burton, 2001, Second Partition, Section 2, Memb. 3, 67). 'The mere act of rising and going, irrespective of whence and whither, did him good' (Beckett, 1974, 35), says 'Pylades', conjuring the Hippocratic saw that walking is the best medicine and the empiricist credo *solvitur ambulando*: it is solved by walking. He offers independent confirmation: 'I have been there again when he returned, transfigured and transformed. It was very nearly the reverse of the Imitation's "glad going out and sad coming in"' (36).

This Orestes is a fugueur rather than a fugitive, his palliative excursions being brief evasions of commitment. The Swiftian lovers' walk beyond Malahide in 'Fingal' confirms that solitary rambling is his only reliable recourse. After indifferent coitus Belacqua, 'a kind of cretinous Tom Jones' (94), sordidly steals away on a bicycle to a pub. 'The simplest form of this exercise was boomerang, out and back' (35), yet even such a barren itinerary can be 'transfigured and transformed':

> Not the least charm of this pure blank movement, this 'gress' or 'gression', was its aptness to receive, with or without the approval of the subject, in all their integrity the faint inscriptions of the outer world. Exempt from destination, it had not to shun the unforeseen nor turn aside from the agreeable odds and ends of vaudeville that are liable to crop up. This sensitiveness was not the least charm of this roaming that began by being blank, not the least charm of this pure act the alacrity with which it welcomed defilement. (36–7)

So unmotivated walking begins in Beckett as a limited therapeutic regimen, a conduit rather than cure for solipsism. Gress is not yet ontological but only remedial and compensatory. Nevertheless, unlike Murphy's malfunctioning rocker and thongs, this exertion readily induces a prolonged anoetic mental state promoting impartial receptivity to mundane happenstance, one uncontaminated by subordination to a paramount rationalizing scheme. Walking is not, as for Rousseau, a coagulant of thought but, as for R. L. Stevenson, its solvent. The pleasure, Stevenson writes in 'Walking Tours', is that 'it gradually neutralises and sets to sleep the serious activity of the mind' (Stevenson, 1946, 143; see Rousseau, 1973, 215). 'Pelorson says he understands Rimbaud who used to compose poems walking', Beckett wrote to Thomas MacGreevy on 8 November 1931. 'But for me, walking, the mind has a most pleasant & melancholy limpness, is a carrefour [crossroads] of memories, memories of childhood mostly, moulin à larmes' [mill of tears] (Beckett, 2009b, 93). The mind itself becomes a footpath along the Dublin hillside songlines that his later work will repeatedly retrace.

Repose by contrast is exposure, as when Belacqua enters a low public-house: 'all the wearisome tactics of gress and dud Beethoven would be done away with if only he could spend his life in such a place' (Beckett, 1974, 40). *Un*welcome defilement comes just when his melancholy 'waits for a sign' (40), in the person of an evangelical pedlar of 'seats in Heaven' (41). The creature's 'deplorable' footwear gives her away: 'the cruel straight outsizes of the suffragette or welfare worker' (41). She too is a seasoned walker, and by devious reckoning cajoles from him enough charity even for his own soul. From the conjunction of a gressive *promeneur* and an aggressive hawker comes *dis*agreeable odds and ends of vaudeville, enough to send chagrined Belacqua back outside to resume his trek 'beyond the river' (43), presumably towards the brothels.

To the solicitations of Christian canvasser and ingénue Belacqua opposes the complacence of the unaccommodated vagrant. Belacqua's vagabondage is however more equivocal and insecure than that of the tinker encountered in 'Walking Out'. Though he has set off aimlessly with a dog on a spring day, the Irish idiom of the title forecasts courtship. His fiancée pursues him on horseback into the woods, probably because Belacqua, 'a kind of cretinous' Leopold Bloom, has proposed a 'cicisbeo' (Beckett, 1974, 94) or *cavaliere servente* to relieve him of conjugal exactions. He thus has all the more cause to revere the resolution and independence of the solitary tinker. Though the vagrant mending a pot beneath his horseless cart growls at the approach of Belacqua, the interloper admires the 'instinctive nobility of this splendid creature for whom private life, his joys and chagrins at evening under his cart, was not acquired, as Belacqua one day if he were lucky might acquire his, but antecedent' (95). So Beckett pricks Irish Protestant contempt for the pariah's fecklessness, a trait associated with Catholics, yet he idealises itinerancy like a Celtic Revival sentimentalist of Catholic poverty, lacquering in picturesque the pauperization of rural labourers. Belacqua 'made an inarticulate flourish with his stick and passed down the road out of the life of this tinker, this real man at last' (95). Like Yorrick's flourish traced down the page of *Tristram Shandy* or the blind piano tuner's tapping in *Ulysses*, Belacqua's prop serves as a surrogate writing implement, its dissolving cursive glyph superseding the verbal and written sign. It does the real talking, bespeaking rugged male solidarity, as though striving for the casual reciprocations of Walt Whitman's 'Song of the Open Road'. The *promeneur solitaire* brandishes an onanistic stand-in in homage to austere male autonomy.

Although Romantic stereotypes are otherwise scorned in the story, the Wordsworthian vagabond, only partially rescued from the Claude glass distortions of aestheticism, remains a paragon. Beckett's leech gatherer is single, unsponsored and free, afoot but not restless, a laconic aristocrat of the pastures and drovers' tracks. The perspective tellingly shifts to the tinker when the fausse-Wordsworthian Lucy ambushes Belacqua. He pleads walking off alone his doldrums (97), but offended by such equivocation she wrings from him a tryst later in another area of the wood. In the interval, unaware that she has meanwhile been struck by a car, Belacqua espies a dancing master and pupil *in flagrante*. The Tanzherr gives chase to the 'creepy-crawly' voyeur, whose feet 'were so raw with one thing and another that even to walk was painful, while to run was torture' (101). Belacqua turns to 'thrust the sharp ferrule at the hypogastreum of his pursuer' (102), but the virile Tanzherr wrests it from the willing wittal and to his lover's rapture pummels him. His weapon forfeited, Belacqua crawls home, but with Lucy now paraplegic the misogynistic Platonist shortly 'is happily married and the question of cicisbei does not arise' (102). The double entendre is as explicit as Irving Berlin's 'My Walking Stick' ('the thing that makes me click on Lovers' Lane') and anticipates the libidinal substitute of 'From an Abandoned Work'. This gear belongs exclusively to male apparel; bourgeois women, even degraded Winnie in *Happy Days*, by contrast sport parasols. In this supremely cynical denouement, there is no further need of walking sticks.

Anticipating the hypertrophied array of Beckett's later stage properties, these expressive, protean and almost purposive walking prostheses become vibrant matter extending or eclipsing the moribunds who grip them (see Bennett, 2010, 21–31 and 89). In the terms of vital materialism, they entangle Beckett's pedestrians among interdependent forces organic and inorganic, which Bruno Latour terms 'actants' or efficacious entities in an environment of indeterminate energies (Latour, 2004, 237). When in *Mercier and Camier* Watt shatters it, Camier grieves for a walking stick aligned with paternity, as the ithyphallic article was bequeathed from his father. In the eighth of the *Texts for Nothing* the beggar's iron-tipped white cane in Place de la République is accorded agency, beating out a memory, even providing a barometer of the season: 'The stick gains ground, tapping with its ferrule the noble bassamento of the United Stores, it must be winter, at least not summer' (Beckett, 1995, 134). His walking articles congruently direct the agency all but forfeited by the infirm pedestrian, who here verges

Figure 6 Marty Rea (Vladimir) and Aaron Monaghan (Estragon) in Druid's Lincoln Center New York production of *Waiting for Godot*, directed by Garry Hynes (2018); Photo Matthew Thompson.

on demotion to mere excipient: 'These insignia, if I may so describe them, advance in concert, as though connected by the traditional human excipient, halt, move on again, confirmed by the vast show windows' (134).

The walking stick, like Estragon's shoes (see Figure 6), Molloy's hat, the greatcoat of the *nouvelles*, Ham's gaff, the sacks of *How It Is*, May's tapping shoes in *Footfalls* (see Figure 10), the ladders of *The Lost Ones* and the djellabas of *Quad* (see Figure 1), is a basic implement of what Andy Clark and David J. Chalmers characterise as extended mind. In opposition to mind-body dualism, the concept of extended mind understands environmental processes to interact necessarily with mental ones to shape human conceptions of the world: 'the human organism is linked with an external entity in a two-way interaction, creating a *coupled system* that can be seen as a cognitive system in its own right' (Clark and Chalmers, 2010, 29). Beckett's pedestrian gear is endued with an active externalism, entering into '*a proper part of some cognitive system*, such as a human agent' (Clark, 2010, 83). These inalienable possessions complement internal affordances to help situate and cohere a porous self where distinctions of inner and outer blur. Once Beckett adds legs to its monadic carapace, the self involves itself in an extended system or what Clark and Chalmers call 'a coupling of biological organism and external resources' (Clark and Chalmers, 2010, 39).

A walking stick is a stylised crutch, remedial for sacrificed quadrupedal equilibrium, but equally an extension of mind. The interaction between Molloy and his pair of crutches delivers cognitive 'rapture':

> There is rapture, or there should be, in the motion crutches give. It is a series of little flights, skimming the ground. You take off, you land, through the thronging sound in wind and limb, who have to fasten one foot to the ground before they dare lift up the other. And even their most joyous hastening is less aerial than my hobble. (Beckett, 1955, 86)

Insignia of infirmity convert into instruments of cognition by this coupling, for by harnessing himself to the device Molloy learns to wield a weapon, launching his legs against a perceived assailant.

Because the crutches help him to attain a certain state of mind, they become constitutive for Molloy. Minds in Beckett are inseparable from the conditions of their embodiment in specific environments and among specific affordances. Olga Beloborodova stresses Beckett's corollary shift from representation to enactment, for in this model cognition is performative, involved in shaping the world in perpetual feedback (Beloborodova, 2020, 28–32). The pedestrial onward imperative in Beckett coincides with the continuous process of consciousness itself. Molloy's sucking stones are at the nexus of brain and environment in part because he alternates the stones while walking, where the interaction between embodied perceiving subject, affordances and the environment is continuous and generative. The body and its objects become coextensive with mental life, which too is gressive.

Even reduced to crawling, Molloy can exult in such a versatile prosthesis. The ignominious seeming reversion to infancy is rehabilitated without recourse to animism or chthonic vitalism. Neither prostrate victim nor stealthy woodkern, Molloy phlegmatically resigns the righteous cranial predominance that upright posture instils to practice instead a lowly perseverance:

> Flat on my belly, using my crutches like grapnels, I plunged them ahead of me into the undergrowth, and when I felt they had a hold, I pulled myself forward, with an effort of the wrists. For my wrists were still quite strong, fortunately, in spite of my decrepitude, though all swollen and racked by a kind of chronic arthritis probably. This then briefly is how I went about it. The advantage of this mode of locomotion compared to others, I mean those that I have tried, is this, that when you want to rest you stop and rest, without further ado. (Beckett, 1955, 121)

Molloy's crawl thus combines the body not only with a tool but with the route itself. The paths Beckett's characters tread further extend prosthetic agency, as affordances as well as symbolic fields. The first human intervention in the

Paleolithic landscape, paths entail natural and cultural isomorphisms across human, organic and inorganic materials that blend ontological categories (see Bennett, 2010, 99). In the Dublin hills and what became Foxrock, primeval herds first beat down the paths that hunters and drovers followed, erecting the Neolithic dolmens of transhumance that were the second intervention, and later the druidic cromleachs and cairns, followed by militias, settlers, merchants, missionaries, surveyors and speculators; along with the communications and utilities infrastructure that, culturally encompassed, determined and underwrote the Becketts' Sunday tramps. This pedestrian coordination is another instance of the cognitive coupling that Clark and Chalmers assert constitutes human thought. The narrator of 'First Love' speculates whether 'it was not rather the path, so iron hard and bossy as perhaps to feel like cobbles to my tread' that prompted his surrender to Anna (Beckett, 1995, 36). Belacqua's walking stick, a talisman against melancholy, augments an insularity of the self that the path then dispels in an interaction of bodies, forces and affordances.

Flânerie, Automatism and Dérive

The walking stick is not in Beckett the flâneur's accessory. Belacqua wields not the cane of urbane male nonchalance but the workaday staff that it supplanted (see Amato, 2004, 89). Belacqua's is a wanderer's weapon, tipped with a ferrule. Mercier's is a crutch: 'He helped himself on by means of a stick with which he struck the ground at every step he took, not at every two, at every one' (Beckett, 1988, 110).

What Edmund White calls 'the great city of the flâneur' (White, 2001, 17), the Paris of Rousseau's *Rêveries* and its Romantic epigones, of Baudelaire, Nerval and Apollinaire, where Dada inaugurated *déambulations* and its Surrealist successors mobilised Freud to slink into the streets' unconsciousness, where Walter Benjamin prowled the last arcades for the hieroglyphs of a pharaonic capitalism, and where the Situationists would soon make drunken *dérives* into the new urbanism, is not the city Beckett walks. 'I was a very slow walker', the choleric wayfarer of 'From an Abandoned Work' confides, employing English equivalents of *flâner*: 'I didn't dally or loiter in any way, just walked very slowly, little short steps and the feet very slow through the air' (Beckett, 1995, 157). A retort to the boast of the New York flâneur Walt Whitman in 'Song of Myself' that 'I loaf and loiter and invite my soul' (Whitman, 1996, 63).

Beckett does not adopt the gait that Éric Hazan in *L'Invention de Paris* and White in *The Flâneur* would make the signal quality of Parisian circulation. To Benjamin, Paris was ideal for the ascetic compulsion of flânerie because its public spaces had the quality of interiors (Benjamin, 1999, 417–20). White says that 'flânerie is the best way to impose a personal vision on the palimpsest of Paris' (White, 2001, 187), where proliferate 'priceless but free memories only waiting for a flâneur to make them his own' (193). He notably never mentions Beckett, whose walkers are dispossessed rather than proprietorial. Though the vagabond of *Mercier et Camier* shares the name of Louis-Sébastien Mercier, who researched afoot his twelve volume *Tableau de Paris* (1788), Beckett's Mercier cannot even be sure of the basic topography of his native city.

In the *Arcades Project* Benjamin, citing flânerie's association with poetry, notes that the artist should look to the strangeness of the everyday by deliriously imagining Paris as Venice (Benjamin, 1999, 436–8). Belacqua's sole sally into flânerie was composed by Beckett in Surrealist Paris in 1932, but describes a Dublin that refuses transmutation into the Florence of Beckett's study trip. Before the Fricas' dreaded party in *Dream of Fair to Middling Women*, Belacqua minutely anticipates perambulation to a pub by 'long straight Pearse St.', which 'permitted of a simple cantilena in his mind' (Beckett, 1993, 201). The *cantilena* tune that orphically lulls his turmoil combines with the Quattrocento-inspired look-out tower of the fire-station (see O'Brien, 1986, 167–9) to transmute the Dublin walk into the Tuscan idyll of a character bearing the name of Dante's Florentine idler:

> For there Florence would slip into the cantilena, the Piazza della Signoria and the No 1 tram and the festival of St John there with the torches of resin ensconced in the niches of every tower flickering all night long and children with the rockets at the fall of night over the Cascine ... .Then he walked slowly in his mind down the sinister Uffizi to the parapets of the Arno etc. This pleasure was bestowed by the knowledge of the Fire Station across the way that had apparently been copied here and there from the Palazzo Vecchio. In homage to Savonarola? Hee! Hee! Anyway, no matter how you looked at it, it was a toleramble ramble in the gloaming. (Beckett, 1993, 202)

Auto-da-fe thereby becomes a harmless joke and even 'painfully' lacerated feet cannot deter the psychogeographical transposition to the Tuscan tune of his 'cerebro-musical-box' (202). Yet the delectable pedestrial trance is abruptly dispelled when 'a terrible thing happened', a pair of importunate associates waylay Belacqua (202). The insular tight-knit capital of ultramontane Eire denies its native son the incognito and autonomy required to assume the suspect antinomian importation of flânerie.

Not even as a traveler could Beckett long fall into the flâneur's humour. The six notebooks he filled with over 120,000 words while traversing Germany from October 1936 until the following March are dominated by minute memoranda of the art he sought out, with few street scenes despite his extensive walking. One such passage shows a flâneur's aesthetic predilection but also an almost agoraphobic estrangement: 'Then by foot to Landungsbrücken & through Elbtunnel', he writes in the 3 November 1936 entry; 'Impressive & nightmarish, especially the Fahrschächten, pits of steel with 6 lifts each & German expressionist film screw stairs. Whole thing somehow kinematic. Hordes of dockers homeward bound on far side, pouring into lifts & clattering down stairs' (qtd in Kaspar, 2007, 67). The entry reveals the fascination with expressionist cinema that decades later he brought to his teleplays for Süddeutscher Rundfunk (see Hartel, 2005 and Veit, 2009). This cinema discounts flânerie, instead pairing the disfigured, disoriented movement of prey with the fixated stalker, which Beckett combines in the doppelgänger of Buster Keaton's Object and Eye in *Film*.[9]

In the 25 October 1936 Hamburg entry Beckett observed that 'the noise of my steps in the leaves reminds me of something, but can't find what' (qtd in Nixon 2011, 115). The memory was of childhood, and decades later he was doing the same thing in Paris, as his friend Anne Atik recalled in the documentary *As the Story Was Told*: 'He loved walking, rue Luxembourg especially. And he loved walking through, shuffling through the leaves, and he said it always reminded him that he did the same thing when he was a boy'. The shuffle reappears in Arsene's recollection of 'children walking in the dead leaves' in *Watt* (Beckett, 2009c, 38), itself an anticipation of the narrow track 'made of dead leaves' in the fifth of the *Fizzles*: 'A reminder of beldam nature. They are dry' (Beckett, 1995, 237). Memory arrives not from sight or reverie but up from his feet, like Proust's Marcel on the cobbles of the Guermantes' courtyard in *Le temps retrouvé*, the tribology that would enter Beckett's dramaturgy. Another Hamburg walk, he noted on 7 November 1936, led him to 'feel most happily melancholy' (qtd in Nixon, 2007, 73). Burton's walking cure does not in Beckett assuage melancholy so much as transmute it into the *bémolisé* key, the '*Wehmutswonne und süßer Schwermutzauber*' of Robert Walser's 'The Walk': the glad and sweetly enchanted melancholy that mingles outside and inside as well as body and mind in aimless pedestrial synaesthesia (Walser, 1985, 55). In terms of examples Beckett esteemed, this is the *Wehmut* not of Albrecht Dürer's seated torpor in *Melencolia* but of its 'pleasures' reached by 'ev'n step and musing gait' in John Milton's 'Il Penseroso' (Milton, 1980, 37).

Baudelairian programmes of purposive literary tourism proved ineffectual to Beckett. The Ohlsdorf cemetery excursion for lyric inspiration only confirmed his lethargy. 'I feel nothing', he admitted in the diary; moving among the graves 'dully and without ad quem [towards which] & without feeling' (qtd in Nixon,

---

[9] For the impact of expressionist cinema on Beckett, see Hartel (2005).

2011, 113 and 114). Failing to kick-start a poem, he decided to write instead an article about the Hamburg cemetery: 'Tone: cold elegiac. Code Napoléon. Precise placings of preposterous Tatsachen [facts]' (113). This variation on the 'cold pastoral' of the much-admired Keats' Grecian urn and the civil code on which Stendhal claimed to base his style also failed, and Beckett waited another decade before turning this deficiency of feeling into his subject, finding the cold elegiac tone in Code Napoléon French and precisely placing the preposterous *Tatsachen* that make up 'Premier amour'. The 1946 *nouvelle* contrasts the 'preferred Ohlsdorf' ramble with the cemetery that the narrator walks to consult his father's grave (Beckett, 1995, 27). 'First Love' is framed by walks to and from fatherhood, 'links' between filial mourning and paternal desertion (25). The protruding belly of his pregnant mate Lulu disrupts a reverie of trails associated with his father (reprising his role of orienting denominator in 'The End'; 98–9):

> She had drawn back the curtain for a clear view of all her rotundities. I saw the mountain, impassible, cavernous, secret, where from morning to night I'd hear nothing but the wind, the curlews, the clink like distant silver of the stone-cutters' hammers. I'd come out in the daytime to the heather and gorse, all warmth and scent, and watch at night the distant city lights, if I chose, and the other lights, the lighthouses and lightships my father had named for me, when I was small and whose names I could find again, in my memory, if I chose, that I knew. From that day forth things went from bad to worse, to worse and worse. (Beckett, 1995, 44)

The uterus is a rival secret cavern, but passible. When Lulu compels him to foresee fatherhood, he retreats into the *locus amoenus* of protracted childhood. What begins in a walk to the father's grave ends in flight from paternity – Beckett's signature 'wombtomb', giving 'birth astride the grave', the mingled funeral and parturition of 'A Piece of Monologue': 'birth was the death of him' (Beckett, 1984, 265). 'As long as I kept walking, I didn't hear them, because of the footsteps': the birth pangs are drowned out by the fleeing father's tread, but 'as soon as I halted I heard them again' (Beckett, 1995, 45). The deadbeat dad must be imagined ever after afoot, not a flâneur but an ancient mariner.

Benjamin's flâneur shuttles between dialectical poles, a werewolf yet also a ragpicker, the last hero of modernity yet also a 'suspect' (*Verdächtiger*) in the terms adapted from his friend Franz Hessel's landmark work of flânerie, *Spazieren in Berlin* (Benjamin, 1988, 420; Hessel 2012, 23–7). He is a dissenter from the Taylorist imperatives of capitalist productivity (see Benjamin, 1974, 679) yet also a mercenary empathizing with exchange value – a capitalist spy 'on assignment in the realm of consumers' (Benjamin,

1999, 427–8). While Beckett's laggards too disdain historiography and philosophy in favour of stark exposition, they are by no means 'priests of the genius loci' (Benjamin, 1988, 416–20) – they are indifferent to surroundings. Neither aesthetes nor scapegraces, the deadbeats eschew politics, refusing participation in society from no principled objection. The baffled tramp in 'The End' recoils from the Leftist proselytiser who glibly reduces his indigence to an illustration of class inequality. Whereas Benjamin's flâneur preserves his personality, Beckett's walker aspires to anonymity, like Object in *Film* scurrying to avoid the perceiving Eye. They withhold their names or the names are ciphers.

The anonymous narrator of 'The Calmative' shares the flâneur's compulsion to circulate idly. 'What possessed me to stir when I wasn't with anybody?', he wonders:

> It was cloudy and cool, I insist, but not to the extent of luring me out. I couldn't get up at the first attempt, nor let us say at the second, and once up, propped against the wall, I wondered if I could go on, I mean up, propped against the wall. Impossible to go out and walk. (Beckett, 1995, 61, 62)

Yet ambulatory automatism overtakes him: he proceeds 'with short steps' (62) and wearing a 'vast cloak' (64) tailored from the heraldic long green greatcoat of his father that in Beckett's personal mythology blazons perished peregrine care. 'I had merely to bow my head and look down at my feet, for it is in this attitude I always drew the strength to, how shall I say, I don't know' (66). Like

Figure 7 Buster Keaton as Object in *Film*.

Maddy's progress in *All That Fall*, the excursion is city pastoral, including entrance through the Shepherds' Gate and an encounter with a barefoot goatherd, all Swiftian satire surprisingly withheld. Details of flânerie multiply: a 'charming' Saxon Stützenwechsel in an organ-resounding cathedral, the panorama from its touristed spire, a cyclist pedalling while reading an open newspaper and ringing his bell, and an apparent prostitute. The goatherd gives the crone a candy and a commercial traveller offers a philtre in exchange for a kiss. His pains magically disappear in an air of casual enchantment akin to Walser's genial pedestrian excurses. He is led inexorably by his feet: 'I thought I could go no further, but no sooner had the impetus reached my legs than on I went, believe it or not, at a very fair pace' (69).

The walk turns increasingly more Bram Stoker than Baudelaire:

> Ah yes, my spoils. I tried to think of Pauline, but she eluded me, gleamed an instant and was gone, like the young woman in the street. So I went in the atrocious brightness, bedded in my old flesh, straining towards an issue and passing them by to left and right and my mind panting after this and that and always flung back to where there was nothing. I succeeded however in fastening briefly on the little girl. (75)

The story's opening no longer seems a bluff: 'I don't know when I died. It always seemed to me I died old' (61). Like 'The End', 'The Calmative' proceeds in the disjunctive registers of pedestrian excursus and eidolopoeia – address of the undead, like the story 'Echo's Bones'. By first light this downmarket Dracula collapses on the street, 'but up with me again and back on the way that was not mine, on uphill along the boulevard' (67).

In Beckett flânerie reverts from genteel sauntering to its primary sense, vagrancy. The narrator's avatar tapping along Place de la République in *Texts for Nothing* is not a flâneur or a Chaplinesque tramp but a deaf hunchbacked beggar. He is imagined as an assemblage of 'dream infirmities' going 'round and round this grandiose square which I hope I don't confuse with the Bastille, until they are deemed worthy of the adjacent Père Lachaise or, better still, prematurely relieved trying to cross over, at the hour of night's young thoughts' (Beckett, 1995, 134). Place de la République is neither adjacent to Père Lachaise a half kilometre down the Avenue de la République, nor easily confounded with the Place de la Bastille. Such spatial uncertainty, however, does not belong to Surrealist delirium or even to the 'Surrealist realism' of Louis Aragon's *Paysan de Paris* (*Paris Peasant*) (Aragon, 1994, xiv), but to oblivious debility. The Surrealists combined Freudian dream psychology with geomancy to redeem undifferentiated place, equating apparent dearth with a brimming unconscious that the legs could trespass and reconceptualise.

Surrealist oneiromancy was a vertiginous exercise in nonpurposive freedom, a subversive mysticism of the everyday. On Beckett's Paris streets the members practiced random walks as a variation on automatic writing in real space. In *Entretiens*, André Breton claims that the absence of aim detached the walk from social reality and revealed the frontier between conscious and dreamed life, releasing phantasms beneath the step. Errancy afforded entrance to prohibited regions of consciousness.

Beckett's kinship with Surrealism extends to translations for Nancy Cunard's *Negro Anthology*, for *transition* and its capitalised successor, for the Surrealist number of *This Quarter*, in which he also published poetry (see e.g. Friedman, 2019, 62–148). He translated the poetry of André Breton and Paul Eluard, signed Eugene Jolas's Jungian manifesto 'Poetry Is Vertical', likely viewed the 1936 London Surrealist exhibition, admired Luis Bunuel and Salvator Dalí's film *Un chien andalou*, and wrote the preface to the Jean Cocteau catalogue for the 1938 Surrealist show of his erstwhile lover Peggy Guggenheim. He translated Eluard's flâneur poem 'La Vue', notably adding a pun to 'Dans une rue très passante' and 'Parmi tant de passants': 'In a most thoroughfare' and 'In a so thoroughfare' (Beckett, 2012, 77, 78, and 368).

The generative imagination that substitutes myth and enchantment for reason and scrutiny, that touts pedestrial access to new energies and the ideal by immersion in ephemera and chance, where Aragon's 'metaphysical entity of places' coheres for those practicing 'ambiguous activities' (Aragon, 1994, 13), can only echo for Beckett the antiquated tenets of the Celtic Twilight. By means of 'simple walks' come metaphysical revelations of the divine for Aragon (184–5), whereas in Beckett not transfiguration but disfiguration ensues. Even his impaired tramp in Place de la République must be promptly recanted as insufficiently degraded, and so is replaced by an old mendicant: 'the old feet shuffle on, towards an even vainer death than no matter whose' (Beckett, 1995, 135).

Beckett's Paris thus does not conceal the 'mythology of the modern' that flânerie reveals to Aragon (Aragon, 1994, xii). The metropolis is usually generic and mundane rather than an enthralling palimpsest. Molloy, who cannot bend his knees, is not pursuing a streetwise gamine to the madhouse, as does Breton in *Nadja*, nor stalking an elusive nubile, as in Philippe Soupault's *Les Dernières Nuits de Paris*, but is crawling home to his senile mother. Though Beckett shares the Surrealist conviction that the contradictions of being are ineluctable, his work mocks their exaltation of eros into augury of this ineffable reality. The title of 'First Love' invokes Leopardi's 'Premio Amore' and Turgenev's novella only ironically. The lover is no cynosure, and eros is neither enduring nor a portal to an occult realm. Walking away from consort and newborn in 'First Love', the cursed progenitor flees not the mystery but the terrible intelligibility of love.

What Beckett got from the Surrealists was not a program for peripatetic automatic writing but for ambulatory automatism. In the 1930s Beckett took copious notes on hysteria and translated Aragon and Breton's encomium 'Hysteria' for the 1932 surrealist special issue of *This Quarter* (see Maude, 2013, 159–61). In the wake of his father's death within the year, and that of his erstwhile lover Peggy Sinclair, he began to suffer from such hysterical symptoms as an arrhythmic heart, panic attacks and even paralysis, like the permanently immobilised listener in *Company*. Breton had been particularly fascinated by the outbreaks of *automatisme ambulatoire* first diagnosed by Jean-Martin Charcot, beginning with the otherwise sober and respectable gas fitter Albert Dadas, a male hysteric who spontaneously embarked on treks from Bordeaux, emerging from amnesia disoriented, penniless and without identity papers in such cities as Marseilles and Moscow. These *fugueurs* held an obvious interest for Beckett, as dromomania, reducing the subject to King Lear's 'poor bare forked animal', eludes diagnosis and thwarts treatment. Ian Hacking, whose analysis of the transitory epidemic of ambulatory automatism, *Mad Travellers*, informs Joshua Ferris's contemporary American update of the Beckettian dromomaniac, *The Unnamed*, affirms the superiority of literature to show 'how our fellow men and women break up, in a time and at a place' (Hacking, 1998, 5). He asserts that 'novelists provide a better model' than diagnosticians and historians of psychiatry, for without intellectual agendas 'they give us suffering and comedy and avoid profundity' (5).

Ulrike Maude describes Beckett's work as a literature of the embodied subject, in which 'the mind is part and parcel of the body and the body infused with memory and intelligence' (Maude, 2015, 182). The mind here is however conditioned by an unruly body, walking never a liberating atavistic reversion to the motor imperative. Beckett made extensive entries into the *Dream Notebook* on the loss of agency in aberrant involuntarily bodily actions; these document what Maude calls the 'sheer terror of being run away with a bodily function' (176). In his work ambulatory automatism does not divulge a cryptic order of authentic being; it does not access the infrastructural unconscious of the city but its vacancy. The profane illumination vouchsafed to Aragon in the condemned Passage de l'Opéra is reduced to Molloy slowly realizing that the dim soiled cul-de-sac he is groping along is really a chapel. No metaphysics of the surface detains here, no hieroglyphs for Aragon's 'modern Champollions' to decipher in mantic threshold states (Aragon, 1994, 164), rather hallucinatory glimpses of primordial biological derangement across what Beckett later termed the brain's 'synaptic chasms' (Beckett, 2016, 506).

This brings Beckett closer to Dadaism, well beyond Lucky's Café Voltaire tirade and dance. Where Surrealists sought the city's veiled meaning, Dada finds triteness and inanity. Ambulatory automatism is not secular divination. The *fugueur* is not mesmeric and has no unconscious to delve. Beckett, who translated Tristan Tzara, shares with Dada contempt for the city's vain self-assertion and mockery of its productions. The group launched its inaugural *déambulation* on 14 April 1921 from Saint Julien le Pauvre because the inconsequence of the quarter served as synecdoche for the meretricious banality of the touristic Paris. Aimless pedestrianism in a marginal district foreswears the picturesque, historical, and sentimental attractions of the city as falsifying bric-a-brac. Francesco Careri writes that Dada 'understood the specular system of industry and tourism to have transformed the city into a simulation of itself, and so they wanted to show its *nothingness*, disclose its cultural void, and exalt its absence of any significance, its banality' (Careri, 2006, 135; my translation). The Dublin of *Molloy* is a Dada travesty, down to its puerile pseudonym Ballybe, the names of its inhabitants and the scatology (cancelled in draft) of its chief industry (see O'Reilly, Van Hulle and Verhulst, 2017a, 381–7).

For the flâneur and Surrealist stalker Beckett substitutes the straggler, who is too flagrantly impecunious to achieve anonymous immersion in the crowd, too apathetic to inventory antiquities and atmospheres, and too cynical to register metaphysical portents. The Beckett walk is not ruminative, demonstrative, or inquisitive. The drifters of his early French fiction practice a Dada regimen of aimless movement within a banal *terrain vide*. 'Where do our feet think they're taking us? said Camier. They would seem to be heading for the canal, said Mercier' (Beckett, 1988, 21). *Mercier and Camier* summarises the pseudo-couple's subsequent exchange: '5. Did what they were looking for exist? 6. What were they looking for? 7. There was no hurry' (23). Though they nominally seek a lost sack associated with salvation ('the said sack contains something essential to our salvation'; Beckett, 1988, 59; 1970a, 94), the 'quest' or 'recherches' (116; 71) is a pretext, for 'only one thing mattered: departure' (24):

> Do you know where we are going? said Camier.
> What does it matter, said Mercier, where we are going? We are going, that's enough. No need to shout, said Camier.
> We go wherever the flesh creeps least, said Mercier. We dodge along, hugging the walls, wherever the shit lies least thick. We stumble on an alley in a thousand, all we need do is pace it to and fro till it's no better than the others, and you want to know where we are going. Where are your sensibilities this evening, Camier? (71)

They are not collecting impressions or botanizing on the pavement: 'We are going, that's enough' (151). The topography of Dublin is elided rather than raked for clues to gnostic patterns of sense. Mercier's hometown promenade in Chapter V turns up two Wordsworthian crones and a brief childhood recollection, otherwise the city is nondescript, its Dublin character further generalised in the original French. Like Murphy 'his being fills again with that merciful fog which is the best he knows, he's good for the long road yet' (132). Nor does the civil guard tolerate promenading. Mercier, Camier and Watt are accosted at once:

> A police constable barred their way.
> This is a sidewalk, he said, not a circus ring.
> What is that to you? said Camier.
> Fuck along with you now, said Mercier, and no nonsense.
> Easy! Easy! said Watt. (112)

'You don't own the sidewalk', the constable declares. Watt assures him that his companions are harmless lunatics, but the constable barks: 'Go and promenade in the country' (113). Further evidence that this French novel does not take place in France.

Beckett's laggards are not scouting in the social margins for frissons of alterity, or for awakening subcultures, or obscured historical vestiges; they indifferently occupy that margin already. They are not collecting impressions or, like the psychogeographer, assembling a dossier. Mercier guides Camier at the end of the novel to view the sunset from a generic bridge of risible touristic pretensions: 'It itself was charming, connoisseurs were heard to say, a charming, charming bridge. Why not? Its name in any case was Lock Bridge, and rightly so, one had only to lean over the parapet to be satisfied on that score' (120). The companions approximate the C. D. Friedrich *Rückenbild* that Beckett would reproduce at the end of both acts of *Waiting for Godot*, but Camier is indifferent first to the bridge prospect and then, near the 'grim pile' of a hospital, to that from the canal, into which he seems poised to drop. As night falls he instead takes his leave of Mercier, who at the end is relieved by the subsiding city bustle: 'he could hear the sounds the long day had kept from him, human murmurs for example, and the rain on the water' (122).

Is this the blasé blunting of discrimination that Georg Simmel characterises as a defence against the tumult of the capitalist city? 'The self-preservation of certain personalities is bought at the price of devaluating the whole objective world, a devaluation which in the end unavoidably drags one's own personality down into a feeling of the same worthlessness' (Simmel, 1950, 415). Though this worthlessness is explicit in Murphy's resort to Geulincx ('*ubi nihil vales, ibi nihil velis*'; Beckett, 1970b, 178) and implicit in Camier's torpor, the dissociation of Beckett's sojourners in the city does not, as for Simmel in 'The Metropolis and

Figure 8 Jack B. Yeats, *The Two Travellers* (1942); Collection Tate Modern.

Mental Life', internalise the levelling of the money economy, for indigence largely excludes them from its illusions. Nor does disassociation prop up the ego, for moral indigence excludes them from its illusions. It is not that the differing value of things has become insubstantial but that the perception of value itself is in ruins.

The Lettrists and successor Situationists responded to this devaluation in Beckett's Paris, and superficially these slackers on a bar crawl approximate Beckettian deadbeats. They however radicalised itinerancy into Marxian critique. They presented themselves not as degenerates but as freelance social scientists on psychogeographic reconnaissance (see Coverley, 2012, 71–2). They were insurgents whose group *dérives* or driftings were ludic and disorienting expeditionary prowls to recuperate the Hausmannised city from commodification, spectacle, mechanization, and the 'capitalist domestication of space' (qtd in Knabb, 2006, 87). Out of the poetic materials of bowery warrens they would assemble an anti-art to subvert the capitalist system with giddy Dadaist insolence, happening upon passional zones uncontaminated by globalizing capital. They practiced insubordination to the designated uses and habitual influences of urban space to affirm autonomy and individuality. Impelled by a negative aesthetic that called language into question and advocated free-form procedures, their *dérives* were rapid 'passages through varied ambiances'

(Knabb, 2006, 52), to discover the conscious and unconscious effects of the built environment on the sensibility of its users, including tones, rhythms, smells. The psychogeographic jaunt they pioneered was both a delirious errancy and a prophetic, inquiring and exorcizing march.

Beckett shared Guy Debord's Schopenhauerisch view of life as aimless 'ontological voyage' (Merrifield, 2005, 143), and they should have crossed paths on their all-night benders. He is 'still drunk', Beckett writes to Barbara Bray on 22 September 1964 after one, and the letter's semantic rupture, as though mimicking the recently published *How It Is*, supplies a sodden insight into Beckett's Parisian promenades as mole-like gropings rather than the 'were-wolf' *flânerie* of Benjamin: 'Out now prowl out soon prowl mind stumble unseeing glare lifetime of' (Beckett, 2014b, 628). Four years later the May days would draw its slogans from Situationist polemics and exalt Debord, but, like Theodor Adorno Beckett was unsympathetic to the revolt.

Although Iain Sinclair, predicating his walk above the Ginger Line in *London Overground* on the geography of *Murphy*, claims Beckett as an unjustly over-looked London walker, he properly refrains from enlisting the novel in the ranks of psychogeography (see Sinclair, 2015, 240–2). Even in October 1962, super-vising a production almost thirty years after his first residency, Beckett suffers 'the horror' of London: '*la vieille frénézie de marche à pied me reprend. Espèce de fuite en rond*': 'the old walking frenzy gets hold of me again. Some sort of escape, walking in circles' (Beckett, 2014b, 510). Not psychogeography but a premonition of walking in a tight circuit in *Quad*.

Beckett had to wait forty years after the Ohlsdorf excursion to compose a cemetery poem, and when he did it was in Tangier, and the result was counter-flânerie and a travesty of the Graveyard Poets. The mirlitonnade 'ne manquez pas à Tanger' sardonically recommends an exile's pathetic plot. In the 'Sottisier' notebook immediately follows its twin, 'ne manquez pas à Stuttgart', which recommends the Neckarstraße precisely because the street's present nullity ('du néant là') arouses the suspicion that it had never been lively (Beckett, 2012, 215).

Nothing is there really to miss in either necropolis, an impression under-scored by the fact that the 1977 poems are immediately preceded in the notebook by a memorandum appropriately parsing the myth of Clotho, Lachesis and Atropos. Pluto's ministers of fate shadow the funereal flâneur, and recto Beckett enters commensurate lines of spectral straggling: 'vieil aller/ vieux arrêts// aller/ absent/ absent/ (s')arrêter'[10] (facsimile in Nixon and Van Hulle, 2017, 178).

---

[10] The reflexive is cancelled in the typescript (facsimile in Nixon and Van Hulle, 2017, 179) and printed version (Beckett, 2012, 216).

Closed Space and Open Road

Because they are deaf to Situationist perambulation, Beckett's closed space texts of the 1960s stand in dialectical relation to the emancipatory polemics launched during Debord's parallel Paris night walks. The texts explicitly depart from ranging peripatetic narrative. No sooner does 'All Strange Away' set another prowler afoot than the narrator retracts the trope: 'Out of the door and down the road in the old hat and coat like after the war, no, not that again. Five square, six high, no way in, none out, try for him there' (Beckett, 1995, 169). These forays into topothesia (description of imaginary space) shift from experiential meanders to serial procedures, yet the withdrawal from figuration in a ground to performative abstraction in strict Euclidian space retains the walking figure. Egress cedes to ingress; walking out to walking in. They notably depart from carceral conventions. While Xavier de Maistre's journeys around a room during house arrest are imaginatively peopled, or convicted Nazi Albert Speer's Spandau Prison yard circuit transposes the milestones of a circumequatorial trek (see respectively *Voyage autour de ma chambre* and *Spandauer Tagebücher*), Beckett devises ruins and rotundas, quadrangles, Kafkaesque burrows and research laboratories.

The Lost Ones borrows rhetorically from behaviourism and social anthropology (as well as Jonathan Swift's parody of the Augustan anticipations of them) to report panoptical investigations into the denuded group activities of languishing or active 'searchers' (Beckett, 1995, 203). This dour ethnography reduces social traffic into formication and individual caprice into mechanisation. A madhouse rubber surface strips the searchers of that vestigial Beckettian

Figure 9 Gaston Carlet's recording apparatus for Étienne-Jules Marey's laboratory (1872).

dignity, the sounded footstep: 'Imagine then the silence of the steps' (203). Helter-skelter human traffic is codified into the cybernetic circulation familiar from modernist urban planning: a scopic rationalisation of movement commanding all variables within a sheer, striated vertical construction. The Situationist demand for a spontaneous, mixed and lateral civic constitution, passional and collective rather than efficient and individualist, is summarily negated. The ingressive closed spaces are also in dialectical relation with Beckett's own egressive open road works. The 1977 BBC2 broadcast *Shades* combined the closed space and the open road in dual scenarios of occult embassy: in *Ghost Trio* an Expressionist manikin traces ghostly emanations in a severely rectilinear setting; in ... *but the clouds* ... a manic noir stalker 'brings home the night' to await a celestial communication.[11]

The story 'Enough' was drafted in the same period as *The Lost Ones*, and it celebrates the nomadism extolled by the Situationist International, but where Debord's point of departure was George Burrows, Beckett's is Dickens. Nell assures her grandfather in *The Old Curiosity Shop* that 'we shall have enough, I am sure we shall', in making an escape on foot from his sinister creditors, though 'she knew not whither they were bound' (Dickens, 1924, 160). In 'Enough', Beckett revises Dickens' peripatetic narrative, to which he alludes directly in the story 'Echo's Bones' (see Beckett, 2014a, 24 and 86), and it is markedly less bleak. Unlike Nell, the young girl is neither stalked nor perishes, and though she must endure separation she is not blighted. The Dickensian ideals of humility, simplicity, and faith that Beckett had drawn from Kempis and Geulincx are footpath virtues.

To the purposive 'round pace', Dickens in 'Shy Neighbourhoods' opposed a walk 'purely vagabond. In the latter state, no gypsy on earth is a greater vagabond than myself; it is so natural to me and strong with me, that I think I must be the descendent, at no great distance, of some irreclaimable tramp' (Dickens, 2000, 119). Pedestrian anonymity is more anaesthesia than panacea. Insomniac Dickens flees London at two a.m. to walk thirty miles to his house at Gad's Hill: 'The road was so lonely in the night, that I fell asleep to the monotonous sound of my own feet, doing their regular four miles an hour. Mile after mile I walked, without the slightest sense of exertion, dozing heavily and dreaming constantly' (118).

Though Nell collapses from hunger, fatigue, and exposure to be tended in her last days by the fortuitously reappearing schoolmaster, walking is almost all she knows of happiness. The shredded shoes are by her deathbed to remind her of

---

[11] A third work on the broadcast, *Not I* combines outer and inner, a disembodied buccal torrent into the ears of a helpless shrugging auditor whose back is turned to the audience.

journeys and to rouse her spirits, and her last dreams are of 'journeyings' (Dickens, 1924, 696). At her tomb her doddering grandfather imagines for them new travels and 'paths not often trodden' (702). In 'Enough' the walk is what the speaker too knows of happiness: 'It is then I shall have lived then or never. Ten years at the very least' (Beckett, 1995, 189). Like Nell's grandfather, the mentor's age is measured by bipedal vigour: he was already 'on his last legs' while 'I on the contrary was far from on my last legs. I belonged to an entirely different generation. It didn't last' (187).

The narrator shares Nell's unconditional fidelity to the elder, proceeding at 'an average speed of three miles per day and night' (185). Even as the crone assumes the 'bow-bent' prospect of Wordsworth's old Cumberland beggar, 'his eyes forever on the ground' (Wordsworth, 1954, 116), abject mendicancy is absent. Though 'we walked in a half sleep' like noctambulist Dickens (Beckett, 1995, 191), Beckett's couple is under neither compulsion nor curse. The walk refutes the mind-body split, the legs enjoying parity with the brain; he 'explained to me that anatomy is a whole' (188). There are no clocks or calendars, time being an attribute of space: 'We did not keep tally of the days. If I arrive at ten years it is thanks to our pedometer' (191). Spatialised and embodied, time is no longer ticks on a dial but steps on a dale.

The couple walks out of the discursive routines of abstract, instrumentalised chronological time to assimilate with the recursive cycles of circadian and seasonal time. The body's felt temporality is vouchsafed to these itinerants, whose plodding, vulnerable, digressive wayfaring deviates from the rapid, prudent, progressive navigation of the goal-oriented striver after preferment and social rewards. In the walks of 'Enough' and subsequent works, time is not a substantive but becomes adverbial, a bipedal relation of manner, circumstance or degree.

In contrast to the torrid meridian of *Happy Days*, the weather is 'eternally mild. As if the earth had come to rest in spring' (191). They rose before dawn 'in this endless equinox' (191), as though crossing a verdant equatorial plateau. 'We lived on flowers' (192). In this version of pastoral, hard primitiveness is unsullied by irony, and they tramp 'several times the equivalent of the terrestrial equator' (188). The couple's adhesiveness even partakes of 'The Song of the Open Road' as Whitman links arms with a companion where the earth is enough ('sufficient'), the walk continuous, unmotivated and remote 'from all formulas'; where the universe itself is a road, 'endless as it was beginningless' (Whitman, 1996, 186).

The pastoral path sheds all socially regulated distinction but that of mentor and disciple: 'we advanced side by side hand in hand. One pair of gloves was enough' (Beckett, 1995, 187). Like the lovers crossing the Alps in

D. H. Lawrence's abandoned work *Mr Noon*, but more compatibly, Beckett's couple spoons, one head 'twined in my hair' while the other 'touched me where he wished. Up to a certain point' (191–2). The couple approaches even the Arcadian licence of Theocritus' *Idylls*, Denis Diderot's *Supplément au Voyage de Bougainville* and Torquato Tasso's *Aminta*: '*S'ei piace, ei lice*' – if it pleases, it's permitted (Tasso, 1962, 26). 'I only had the desires he manifested. [...] When he told me to lick his penis I hastened to do so. I drew satisfaction from it. We must have had the same satisfactions. The same needs and the same satisfactions' (Beckett, 1995, 186). Navigation cedes to random walk, story to digression, and the acolyte acquires the master's serene defactoism: 'All was. This notion of calm comes from him. Without him I would not have had it' (192). This calm proceeds from the footsoles as an affective and moral dividend of purposeless walking.

Though seemingly a bucolic fancy, the couple's serenity has precedents among long-distance walkers. 'Walking means precisely resigning yourself to being an ambulant forward-leaning body', Frédéric Gros writes. 'But the really astonishing thing is how that slow resignation, that immense lassitude gives us the joy of being. Of being no more than that of course, but in utter bliss' (Gros, 2014, 187). Beckett, substituting '*posa*' for '*gode*' in the Italian walking proverb, would prefer 'rest' to this 'joy' and 'bliss', but resignation is especially apt to 'Enough'. The resignation not of defeat or diminishment but of an earlier young female hiker, Dorothy Wordsworth, resting with William above Grasmere at Hollins Wood on 30 April 1802. 'I lay with half shut eyes, looking at the prospect as in a vision almost I was so resigned to it' (Wordsworth, 1991, 92). She adapts this distinctive Lakes District usage[12] to denote a serene acquiescence or equanimity. As in a vision almost of enough. 'Every year I've got less and less, and every year I'm a happier man', the retired NASA technician M. J. Eberhart, who with ever less gear walked every major American trail, told Robert Moor. The author of the hiking memoir *Ten Million Steps* added, 'I just wonder what it's going to be like when I don't have anything' (Moor, 2016, 324–5). Age, slender means and vulnerability do not markedly expose Eberhart to jeopardy: 'I've been out there so long and so far, by myself, and never felt more at peace and more secure and more in my element. It's not an adrenaline pump or anything like that. It's a resignation just to let it be the way it's going to be' (326). This is the resignation of 'Enough': not the heroic fortitude that boasts of obstacles overcome but placid submission to onwardness.

In Martin Heidegger's vocabulary such lassitude becomes *Gelassenheit* before being, but Beckett does not share Heidegger's conviction that *Dasein*

---

[12] A usage noted in 1897 by the *Journals'* first editor, William Knight (see Wordsworth, 1991, 223).

will show forth. The achieved work of art is not a consummate manifestation of being, as for Paul Celan (whose poem 'Todtnauberg' walks with Heidegger to no such consummation); nor does it bear witness to something beyond itself, as for Czeslaw Milosz; nor is it sacramental, as for David Jones. In contrast to these contemporaries, for Beckett the valid work of art is the scrupulous record of a vain struggle to manifest being – an ongoing march 'on' to being. In 'Pour Avigdor Arikha', the art object is shuttling infantry tracks ('*traces*') observed during a truce before a vast no-mans-land: 'Trêve á la navette et traces de ce que c'est que d'être et d'être devant' ('Truce for a space and the marks of what it is to be and be in the face of') (Beckett, 1983, 152). This quixotic tactic to gain what is not syntactic is repeated right up to Beckett's last story 'Stirrings Still': its unstillable walker in heraldic old coat and hat 'moved on through the long hoar grass resigned to not knowing where he was or how he got there or where he was going or how to get back to whence he knew not how he came' (Beckett, 1995, 263). Only by resigning the need to know might Beckett's walker possibly discover 'the way out. A way out' (260). 'The back roads' that the man shuttles on foot and in reverie grade to an aimless agnostic *on*tology, its tonic chord 'so on': 'So on unknowing and no end in sight. Unknowing and what is more no wish to know nor indeed any wish of any kind' (260 and 263).

The serenity that 'comes from simply following the path' Gros connects 'with the slowness of walking, its absolutely repetitive character' and its potential hiatus from social obligations, passions and goals (Gros, 2014, 145–6). These goals 'are supplanted in the end by the implacable lassitude of walking: just walking. Serenity is the immense sweetness of no longer expecting anything, just walking, just moving on' (146). Excepting Gros's glucose, the continental drifting of 'Enough' walks on past all expectation, a *dérive* Beckett had long idealised. Having purchased Jack Yeats's *A Morning*, Beckett wrote to MacGreevy on 7 May 1936, 'It is nice to have Morning on one's wall that is always morning, and a setting out without the coming home' (Beckett, 2009b, 334). This allusion to Thomas à Kempis' phrase in the *Imitatio Christi* Beckett often recalled, as in the 'German Diaries': the 'glad going out & sorrowful coming home' (Nixon, 2011, 8). The *traces* of 'Enough' entail accord with earthly onwardness. Gros summons the Beckettian formula of *rien à faire*: 'When you have set off for the day, and know that it will take so many hours to reach the next stage, there's nothing left to do but walk, and follow the road. *Nothing else to do*' (Gros, 2014, 145; emphasis in original). The narrator's resignation in 'Enough' survives the inexplicable breach from her companion and sustains the equanimity of the narrative: 'Nothing but the two of us dragging through the flowers. Enough my old breasts feel his old hand' (Beckett, 1995, 192).

Thinking on One's Feet: Distributed Cognition

Enough just moving on, for walking is not only the best remedy in Hypocrites' axiom but also restores the body's usurped function in cognition. 'We are not just minds immobile in the silent vat of our skulls', contends Shane O'Mara in his neuroscientific encomium to walking: 'we are minds in movement' (O'Mara, 2019, 61). The minds in pedestrian movement in Beckett cannot gainsay it. Consciousness, even his seediest solipsists discover, issues not from an aloof executive cerebration but from the learned effects, distributed across an activated nervous system and its prostheses, of changes in the environment (see Clark and Chalmers, 2010, 29; Noë, 2009, 142 and 186). The cooperation of somatic and mental apprehension dissolves the inner–outer split and extends cognition over the articulated length of the body. Beckett's often impaired walkers closely perceive gradients and uneven surfaces, obstacles and changing weather and light, all of which dislodge fantasies of an ensconced mind. Their walking dispels the notion of Cartesian cognition for it puts the brain into quickened relation with the thinking body. Their legs often defy subordination to the

Figure 10 Charlotte Emmerson in Richard Beecham's Jermyn Street theatre London production of *Footfalls* (2021).

physiological regime of the brain and poise cognition along the juncture of body, mind and locality.

This embodiment is moreover interdependently situated. The paths of *Nohow On* and the apparel to walk them become not only a means but a contingent property acting upon the characters' minds, conditioning the style and determining the form. To George Duthuit on 9 March 1939, Beckett praised Bram van Velde's perceived effort to paint beyond the false dichotomy of inner and outer: 'ce qu'on appelle le dehors et le dedans ne font qu'un' ('what we call the outside and the inside are but one'); 'Il est dedans, est-ce la même chose ? Il les est, plutôt, et elles sont lui, d'une façon pleine' ('He is inside, is that the same thing? Rather, he is them, and they are him, in a full way'; Beckett, 2011, 136). The anthropologist Tim Ingold writes that 'the ground of knowing – or, if we must use the term, of cognition – is not an internal neural substrate that *resembles* the ground outside but *is itself* the very ground we walk' (Ingold, 2015, 48). He urges that 'cognition should not be *set off* from locomotion, along the lines of a division between head and heels since walking is itself a form of circumambulatory knowing' (Ingold, 2011, 46).

Where however the social scientist Ingold cannot readily forgo the validation of knowledge, the Beckett walk surpasses it. Not knowhow but 'nohow on' (Beckett, 1996, 89). 'What possessed you to come?', the first of the *Texts for Nothing* asks itself; 'Unanswerable, so that I answered, To change, or It's not me, or Chance, or again, To see, or again, years of great sun, Fate'. But these rationalizations are exhausted cultural clichés:

> To change, to see, no, there's no more to see, I've seen it all, till my eyes are
> blear, nor to get away from harm, the harm is done, one day the harm was
> done, the day my feet dragged me out that must go their ways, that I let go
> their ways and drag me here, that's what possessed me to come. (Beckett,
> 1995, 101–2)

The atavistic locomotive compulsion overrides ratiocination, just as the foetus initiates bipedal motions before the cerebral cortex even forms. Equally *ars poetica* and *ars vitae*, this automatism undoes the providential gait of *Pilgrim's Progress*.

The walk also provides an ontological foothold for characters on the verge of evanescence. In 'Stirrings Still' the immobile protagonist 'saw himself rise and go' on silent feet that reinforce his spectrality: 'his soundless tread as when barefoot he trod his floor' (Beckett, 1995, 259, 263). The widow of 'Ill Seen Ill Said' vanishes along with her steps in the snow: 'Slowly she disappears. Together with the trace of her steps' (Beckett, 1996, 68). While the voice of Henry's wife Ada in the 1959 BBC radio broadcast *Embers* may be an hallucination, Henry himself, although equally a figment of radio frequency, is ontologically secure, because, even before his voice is heard, his tread is:

> [*Henry's boots on shingle. He halts. Sea a little louder.*] HENRY: On. [*Sea. Voice louder.*] On! [*He moves on. Boots on shingle. As he goes.*] Stop. [*Boots on shingle. As he goes, louder.*] Stop! [*He halts. Sea a little louder.*] Down. [*Sea. Voice louder.*] Down! [*Slither of shingle as he sits.*] (Beckett, 1984, 93)

Like Maddy's shuffle in *All That Fall*, the audible onwardness of Henry, the crunching tribology of his boot over shingle, confers the mass and momentum that radio elides. The boots are ontological metonyms, a tactile as well as acoustic imprint. This sensory plenitude contrasts with wraithlike Ada: '[*No sound as she sits.*]' (Beckett, 1984, 97) No legs, feet, haunches, ergo a spectre, like the Woman's Voice in *Eh, Joe* or the telekinesis of *Ghost Trio*. To be is to beat a path, even if only to beat a retreat, like Buster Keaton's O in *Film* or the deadbeats of the *nouvelles* (see Figure 7). To Charles Juliet Beckett stressed 'l'importance du pas de l'homme, de nos pas sur cette terre : "Toujours ce va-et-vient [. . .] ce bruit des pas"' ['the importance of man's footstep, of our footsteps upon this earth: "Always this coming and going, this din of footsteps"'] (Juliet, 1986, 47–8; my translation).

In *Footfalls*, which he was drafting at this time, May's step imprints an otherwise precarious existence. In a 1976 letter Beckett tells the actress Billie Whitelaw: 'The pacing is the essence of the matter, to be dramatised to the utmost. The text what pharmacists call excipient' (Beckett, 2016, 424). '*Steps: Clearly audible rhythmic tread*', signals a direction (Beckett, 1984, 239; see Figure 10). Sandpaper was attached to Whitelaw's ballet slippers for the London Royal Court Theatre premiere, which Beckett assisted (Knowlson, 1996, 624). The 'clearly audible rhythmic tread' of the body surpasses speech, now treated as a secondary vehicle for the kinetic matter. May, 'revolving it all' in her mind (240 and 243), revolves too her body at the ends of her strip. 'Watch how feat she wheels', puns the voice of her unseen invalid mother (241).

By graph and stage direction, Beckett indicates every step, noting even by which leg May launches herself along the metre-long track. He adjusted Whitelaw's gait from the original seven paces to nine. May too has made adjustments, having had the carpet removed: 'I must hear the feet, however faint they fall. The mother: The motion alone is not enough? May: No, mother, the motion alone is not enough, I must hear the feet, however faint they fall' (241). As May's steps slow over the course of the play, the light dims and the chime rings more faintly, until in the fourth and final interval the stage is vacant. For his 1976 production of *Tritte* at the Schiller-Theater Werkstatt in West Berlin, Beckett further modified the steps, turns, and pauses in symmetrical relation to the duration of the knell and the glow in order to reinforce May's evanescence between gleams. '*No trace of MAY*': the direction literalises the pedestrian trope that governs a play organised by bipedal trace (243). As her pace, so her being ebbs.[13]

Like Wordsworth pacing the level gravel walk at Dove Cottage, May composes afoot, a mobile contrast to Hamm inditing from a wheelchair or the crone in 'Rockaby'. The pedestrian and the poet converge in the abortive tale of alter ego Amy, who insists 'I was not there' at Evensong (243). May falls silent as her footfalls diminish, the dimmed stage finally housing only a vacancy. Walking and writing ('as the reader will remember', she says; 243) are elided; as in Beckett's *navette* 'mirlitonnade', the shuttling equates *parcours* and page (see Beckett, 2012, 211–12). The shuttle also spatialises the Latin root of ambiguity: an uncertain back and forth movement (*ambigo, ambiguus*). However decisive May's tread, its import, like that of the play's action, remains performatively ambiguous.

'These Wanderings': A Rhetoric of Walking

In 'Conversation about Dante', Osip Mandelstam writes: 'The *Inferno* and especially the *Purgatorio* glorify the human gait, the measure and rhythm of walking, the foot and its shape' (Mandelstam, 2004, 224). The subject of his widow Nadezhda's memoir *Hope against Hope*, which Beckett admired, the poet commends in Dante's prosody a pedestrian rhythm that Beckett emulated. The step, Mandelstam asserts, 'Dante understands as the beginning of prosody', observing that 'in Dante philosophy and poetry are forever on the move, forever on their feet' (107). Mandelstam anticipates Beckett's insistence on the provisional, fluctuating and elastic nature of an aesthetic medium founded on bipedal movement: 'Poetic speech creates its tools on the move and in the same breath does away with them' (144). Beckett's art of recension renders overt this operation, often in explicitly peripatetic terms and contexts: 'Careful. On' (Beckett, 1996, 50).

---

[13] Beckett's scenario has literary precedent in W. H. Davies' *The Autobiography of a Supertramp*: 'My grandfather, with his old habits, would pace slowly up and down the half dark passage, shutting himself out in the cold [...]. When this was done, the old lady would sometimes say, rather peevishly, "Francis, do sit down for a minute or two". Then he would answer gruffly, but not unkindly, "Avast there, Lydia", closing the door to begin again his steady pacing to and fro' (Davies, 1926, 9). For May's compulsion as traumatic symptom and tonic, see Tranter (2018, 156–61).

For Mandelstam, 'to speak means to be forever on the road' (Mandestam, 2004, 115). Beckett's Parisian contemporary Michel de Certeau adapts this homology between bipedal and verbal articulation, joint and tongue, influentially identifying 'walking as a space of enunciation' (Certeau, 1988, 98). 'There is a rhetoric of walking' (100) that, he claims, expresses tacit modes of everyday resistance to technocratic functionalist rationality and the scopic disembodiment of capitalism. As 'the pedestrian speech act' alters spatial elements in a 'phatic' embodiment (98), story becomes an analogous spatial practice to Certeau, preceding and preparing social practices: narratives 'organise walks. They make the journey, before or during the time the feet perform it' (115–16).

In Beckett, story and composition make a dual journey. In particular, his works of non-programmatic *écriture à processus* mimic the process of walking to approach the image in the condition of its emergence. Kinesis enters mimesis, and story becomes stroll. In his only lightly emended draft of *Molloy*, Beckett replaced a meta-textual reference to 'ce récit' ('this narrative') with 'cette promenade' (Beckett, 1982a, 86; see O'Reilly, Van Hulle and Verhulst, 2017a, 218). Though sacrificing this direct allusion to Rousseau's *Rêveries*, he retained the collusion of errancy and narration in the translation: 'these wanderings' (Beckett, 1955, 111). 'I invented it all', admits *The Unnamable*, 'in the hope it would console me, help me to go on, allow me to think of myself as somewhere on a road, moving, between a beginning and an end, gaining ground, losing ground, getting lost, but somehow in the long run making headway. All lies' (Beckett, 1958a, 36). Narration like ontology must abandon the pretence of a teleology in favour of dawdling promenade. 'The essential is never to arrive anywhere, never to be anywhere' (71).

The isomorphism that Certeau and Mandelstam discern between pedestrian and narrative impetus organises a range of Beckett's texts, as when narrative wandering coincides with the widow's 'straying' in the meadow of 'One Evening' (Beckett, 1995, 253). 'Not too fast', the narrator twice enjoins himself (253, 254), narrative becoming as tentative and lumbering as her uncertain gait. The wish 'to put it vaguely' (253) unites indeterminate step and story – more starkly in the original: 'c'est vague' (Beckett, 1976, 63), from the verb *vaguer*, 'to wander' (Latin *vagus*). In the margins of a draft of *Happy Days* Beckett reminds himself to 'vaguen' descriptions of the set (see Gontarski, 1977, 36). The narrator of the counter-pilgrimage novel *How It Is* reminds himself to 'leave it vague leave it dark' – 'ça laisser vague dans l'ombre' (Beckett, 1964, 74; 1961, 92). Vagueness is inevitable where being evades nomination. 'We don't know what our being is', Beckett told Ruby Cohn while staging *Warten auf Godot* in West Berlin (qtd in Cohn, 2006, 134). Vagueness is not a defect to correct but an expressive means and above all a constituent feature of finite embodiment, thus parallel to pedestrial wandering.[14] The lines made from walking divagate, preserving the peripatetic nature both of their matter and inscription.

The rhetorical provisionality maintains the tone of the journal entry, sketch or redaction. Beckett's excursive narrative is draft that stays draft. Throughout *Worstward Ho* and the 'mirlitonnades', the deictic pace of the prosody seeks phatic and rhythmic coincidence with the speaker's aimless steps ('allant sans but'; Beckett, 2012, 216):

> écoute-les
> s'ajouter
> les mots
> aux mots
> sans mot
> les pas
> aux pas
> un à
> un (Beckett, 2012, 211)

In the English version of the *navette* 'mirlitonnade' movement and speech coincide: 'again gone/ with what to tell/ on again/ retell' (Beckett, 2012, 222). Mark Nixon notes in the sequence 'Beckett's repeated use of the image of footsteps, which he compared to the process of writing in that both leave traces' (Nixon, 2006, 99). The deictic approximation of language to thought and experience that Roger Gilbert identifies in the walking poem (and that is already explicit in the gamboling iambic tetrameter of Thomas Traherne's poem 'Walking')[15] exposes the perceiving body to flux (Gilbert, 1991, 23). In *Worstward Ho* Beckett will put language as well as its human figures on the road, composing and decomposing representation. So close is the conjunction of bipedal and prosodic pace that Beckett balked at translation of the story and most of the verses.

Walking Myth and Allegory

The walk supplies Beckett with a primordial spatial figure for laborious passage through time. While the earlier work disrupts the progressive teleology of the journey myth, the later work wants to get to the walk before theology and philosophy do, almost before myth does. For Hans Blumenberg, another contemporary published by Suhrkamp, the pre-conceptual fictive objects of myth provide orientation to the disoriented and anxious mind (see *Paradigms for a Metaphorology* [1960] and *Work on Myth* [1985]), while for Beckett this is

---

[14] In a 1938 review Beckett stated that 'art has nothing to do with clarity, does not dabble in the clear and does not make clear' (Beckett, 1983, 94).

[15] 'To *walk* is by a Thought to go;/ To move in Spirit to and fro' (Traherne, 1965, 189).

a bromide. He both harnesses the walking myth and evacuates it as the basis for an alternative myth, in which the walk undergoes a world of irredeemable contingency. To Charles Juliet he said, 'c'est par la forme que l'artiste peut trouver une sorte d'issue. En donnant forme à l'informe' [it's by the form that the artist can find a way out. In giving form to the formless] (Juliet, 1986, 28; my translation). Directing the 1975 Schiller-Theater production of *Warten auf Godot*, he told the company that the aesthetic aim was 'to give a form to the confusion': 'der Konfusion eine Gestalt zu geben' (qtd in Asmus, 1979, 318). The footpath is in his work among the most expedient of such forms.

In the 18 January 1937 entry of his German diary, Beckett dismisses Walter Bauer's contemporary novel *Die notwendige Reise* (*The Necessary Journey*): 'Journey anyway is the wrong figure. How can we travel to that from which one cannot move away. *Das notwendige Bleiben* [the necessary staying put] is more like it' (qtd in Nixon, 2011, 97). While embarked on his *unnotwendige Reise*, Beckett in the same entry recoils from the 'heroic, the nosce te ipsum, that these Germans see as a journey' (qtd in Nixon, 2011, 73). The previous summer Beckett had read *Faust*, impatient with Goethe's moral uplift (see Van Hulle 2006). On 19 August 1936 he wrote to MacGreevy, 'I can understand the "keep on keeping on" as a social prophylactic, but not at all as a light in the autological darkness' (Beckett, 2009, 386). 'The tensions between the notion of "keeping on" and the impossibility of doing so was later expressed in the last line of *L'Innommable*', write Nixon and Van Hulle (2017, 196). However, stillness – *rigor vitae*, as he quips – proves no more feasible, nor is any 'light into the autological darkness' possible.

Beckett's post-war peregrines consequently do not walk from ignorance to knowledge, and passage takes precedence over destination. In *Molloy*, he travesties the trope of life as a directed journey, yoking *Le Conte du Graal* to Kafka's *Das Schloß* (he read *The Castle* in German) at the expense both of the Grail imagery that T. S. Eliot's notes to *The Waste Land* magnified and of the Homeric analogies that Stuart Gilbert's study of *Ulysses* inflated (see Rabinovitz, 1979, 23–44). Molloy compares his progress to a Calvary with unlimited stations and no hope of Golgotha. Extricating himself from the Fisher-King fortress of Lousse, this mock-Perceval forgoes the quest for mother in favour of gress: 'Not knowing where I was nor consequently what way I ought to go I went with the wind. And when, well swung between my crutches, I took off, then I felt it helping me, that little wind blowing from what quarter I could not tell' (Beckett, 1955, 80).

Soon Molloy adopts the customary stratagem of Beckett's tramps of simply following the sun, pursuing 'a straight line' that only takes him off course (87). A later impulse to seek again his mother drives him to crawl out of a forest, where a ditch and a moor bar any advance.[16] The mechanics of failing locomotion eclipse its goal. Having heard 'that when a man in a forest thinks he is going forward in a straight line, in reality he is going in a circle, I did my best to go in a circle, hoping in this way to go in a straight line' (115). Molloy loses toes like a polar explorer, and while one leg stiffens the other shortens, the sequence outlined exhaustively. Unable any longer to support himself on the exhilarating crutches, he uses them as grapnels to crawl through the forest. This 'veritable calvary' (105) or *via dolorosa* is slow going through the woods: 'Some days I advanced no more than thirty or forty paces' (112). Compulsory intervals of rest increase: 'it was the only way to progress, to stop' (105). Moran's dual journey repeats the aporias of Molloy's, though now in the key not of quest romance but of its seedy generic double the detective fiction. The grail is not a thing but thinglessness, an ascetic evacuation of possessions on a recursive round.

Figure 11 William Blake, illustration to *Pilgrim's Progress* (1824).

---

[16] Though the incipit, which Beckett wrote last, announces his restoration to his mother's domicile, a cognitive and narrative ellipsis obscures the last leg of the journey (see O'Reilly, Van Hulle and Verhulst, 2017, 33).

Protestant allegory lends Beckett a closer walking mythology to complement and confound. If Bunyan's faith could not be defended, *Pilgrim's Progress* was irrefutable. Beckett strips the tidy repertoire of Bunyan's objects of their force as metaphorical tokens in order to charge them with elementary metonymic import, such as when he transforms the flies in *Act without Words I* into a *diabolus ex machina*. So Christian's onerous sack, borne like the Cross of Original Sin (see Bunyan, 1987, 35 and Figure 11), appears in *Mercier and Camier* and then as the infantry haversack of trudging Pim in *How It Is*. Camier insists to Mercier that they return to town to retrieve their sack from an intuition 'that the said sack contains something essential to our salvation. But we know that is not so', said Mercier (Beckett, 1988, 59). What for Christian is a providential disencumbering of the sack is an aporia to the pseudocouple: 'This thing we think we need, said Camier, once in our possession and now no longer so, we situate in the sack, as in that which contains. But on further thought nothing proves it is not in the umbrella, or fastened to some part of the bicycle. All we know is we had it once and now no more. And even that we don't know for sure' (60).

'Dark clouds bring waters': Bunyan allegorically defends the clarifying obscurity of allegory (Bunyan, 1987, 4, 58), whereas Beckett dims his portentous figures. Pozzo and Lucky arrive like the emblems conjured by the Interpreter as moral personifications for Christian's benefit (see Bunyan, 1987, 30), but they baffle stable signification. The pair of prodded clowns in Beckett's *Act without Words II* enacts the dichotomy in *Pilgrim's Progress* of Christian and Sloth (the latter parallel with Dante's lethargic Belacqua). The spry first mime briskly rises to the providential prod and shifts forward his well-equipped sack, while the lethargic second one lags, scarcely able to nudge his sack before slumping into it again. The journey of *Pilgrim's Progress* is shorn in Beckett of purposiveness or justification, but not of typological intelligibility: the inching twins are crude existential personifications. Christian's sack is now a habitation, both a defiled theological symbol and an unsparingly literal version of the vagrant's sidewalk sleeping bag. Lucky's pair of suitcases is a dual emblem of menial and moral servitude: like Christian's sack, they contain no provisions, indeed only sand, but Pozzo's slave foresees no disburdening end to the journey. Vladimir and Estragon are types who play Bunyan's Patience and Passion to Pozzo's despotic Apollyon. 'Thou art one of my subjects, for all that country is mine', blustering Apollyon professes (52), while under the same pretence Pozzo accuses the pair of trespassing his lands. As Christian searches for his misplaced 'roll' of election (41), so the pair awaits Godot's summons to redemption.

And as Christian flees the cries of wife and children at the beginning of *Pilgrim's Progress*, so the narrator flees the cries of wife and newborn child at the end of 'Premier amour': 'Tant que je marchais je ne les entendais pas, grâce au bruit de mes pas' (Beckett, 1970c, 55). Spiritual grace facetiously enters the gait, only to be retracted when a quarter century later Beckett translated the story: 'As long as I kept walking I didn't hear them, because of the footsteps' (Beckett, 1995, 45).[17] Walking offers the fugitive not passage to redemption but periodic sedation from condemnation. Charity may clear Christian's conscience of abandonment, but not this reprobate's conscience. In *Embers* Henry commands hooves to drown out the surf where his father drowned himself: 'Train it to mark time! Shoe it with steel and tie it up in the yard, have it stamp all day! [*Pause.*] A ten-ton mammoth back from the dead, shoe it with steel and have it tramp the world down! Listen to it!' (Beckett, 1984, 93)

Bunyan's belongs to 'the ancient voice' (Beckett, 1964, 7), that composite of inherited culture that reverberates throughout *How It Is*. This contested authority may be estranged, misheard, missaid or ineffable, but it is also indomitable. *Pilgrim's Progress* can be neither escaped nor denied. As Christian so Beckett's Pim must wade through quagmire and ditch in a 'procession' of interchangeably sadistic scapegraces and masochistic scapegoats observing 'a regimen of grace' (Beckett, 1964, 124). The tonal register lurches unpunctuated between trench warfare testimony, actuarial audit and the Book of Common Prayer: 'I go on zigzag give me my due conformably to my complexion present formulation seeking that which I have lost there where I have never been' (46–7). The same instability attaches to the sack, 'sole good sole possession' (8), punning on the Platonic good of the soul. Calvinist burden, soldier's receptacle, Jacob's pillow, teddy-bear, and like Bunyan's allegory venerable despite obsolete:

> no the truth is this sack I always said so this sack for us here is something more than a larder than a pillow for the head than a friend to turn to a thing to embrace a surface to cover with kisses something far more we don't profit by it in any way any more and we cling to it I owed it this tribute. (66)

The sack can be coveted for its release from utility, the very property of Calvinist grace noted a few pages earlier: that some sacks burst while 'others never is it possible the old business of grace in this sewer' (61). The sacks appear to belong to a providentially 'regulated' and 'mathematical' Christian social welfare that thus constitutes 'our justice' (112): 'a love who all along the track at the right places according as we need them deposits our sacks' (138). The 'closed curve' deasil course is universal, as is the mode of

---

[17] The translation of the ending of 'Mal vu mal dit' reverses the substitution: 'Le temps d'aspirer ce vide. Connaître le bonheur' (Beckett, 1981, 76); 'Grace to breathe that void. Know happiness' (Beckett, 1996, 86).

locomotion: 'all is identical our ways and way of faring right leg right arm push pull' (117 and 112). Whether, however, all may obtain grace or Pim be the 'sole elect' is unknown (13), and the self-consuming narrative culminates not in spiritual deliverance but textual disavowal.

In a genetic study of *How It Is*, Anthony Cordingley writes that Beckett 'seeks to deny his texts the capacity to affirm its referents and confer upon them a foundational role yet all the while relying upon them for its meaning' (Cordingley, 2018, 181). Allusion to Bunyan functions neither by parody and pastiche to discredit tradition in its own terms, as in postmodernism, nor discovers in those terms occult orders of transcendent meaning, as in Christian allegory. Cordingley identifies 'an ethical commitment to *go on*' (40), but this goes on too in language. The narrator-narrated of *How It Is* follows the wayward trail of speech: 'words my truant guides with you strange journeys' (Beckett, 1964, 92). Style too walks: the novel's monosyllabic, monotonic, saccadic phrases in unpunctuated discrete paragraphs approximate a phatic enunciation, the slow plod to an ever-receding Celestial City. Decades after deriding the tendency to see life as a journey, Beckett was still depicting life as a journey, not however a pilgrim's progress but pilgrim's gress: a penitential circuit or existential 'pensum' stripped of moral uplift, gnostic comprehension and spiritual teleology.

The Beckett walk is not anagogic but planar: not allegorical ascending stations but contiguous level grades; less metaphoric than metonymic. In Beckett's quixotic search for a walk primitive to myth, symbol and philosophy, the Bunyan progress cedes to the Heraclitus regress. By taking a path one enters and inflects a recursive network, introducing a new circuit inside an established one. The road up and down is one and the same, and in his 'Philosophy Notes' Beckett recorded in his twenties the aphorism of Heraclitus that he would depict in various permutations, including the circuits of *Molloy*, the endless round of *How It Is*, the loop of 'The Way', and the monkish formication of *Quad*: 'The "way up" (earth – water – fire) and "way down" (fire – water – earth) are one and the same, forever being traversed in opposite directions at once, so that everything consists of two parts, one travelling up, the other down' (Beckett, 2020, 46). 'In this ceaseless transformation of all things nothing individual persists', Beckett notes, 'but only the order, in which the exchange between the contrary movements is effected – the law of change, which constitutes the meaning and worth of the whole. The Becoming of Heraclitus produces no Being, as the Being of Parmenides no Becoming' (43).

Beckett adopts Heraclitus's path or track as choice trope of this order. The four cowled pacers of *Quad I* follow a synchronised zigzag around an invisible barrier 'supposed a danger zone. Hence deviation' (Beckett, 1984, 293). A carceral regimen segues into a contemplative askesis suggested by the monastic garb, cloistral layout, Cistercian muteness and sutra instrumentation. While the routine is algorithmic, the tread is choreographic, grounding the enigmatic performance in elemental action. The stage dimensions are measured not in abstract meters but bodily strides: 'Length of side: 6 paces' (291). The pianissimo percussion is 'intermittent in all combinations to allow footsteps alone to be heard at intervals', and each player's celibate step is individuated by a distinct resonance (292 and 293). In the more penitential *Quad II* (see Figure 1) the instrumentation and colour have gone but not the audible constancy of the players' now slower tread, sign of an unspoken pact: 'footsteps only sound' (294). They continue to proceed as though around an unmarked shrine in fulfilment of a vow to walk off a collective burden.

Beckett conceived of a supplementary loop during the Süddeutscher Rundfunk production of *Quadrat* in Stuttgart in May 1981. 'The way wound up from foot to top and thence on down another way', he writes in 'The Way' (Beckett, 2009a, 125; see Figure 12). In the original draft he condenses the axiom: 'The two ways were one way' (xi), rivalling Heraclitus's pithy phrasing (or that of Hippolytus quoting the fragment in *Refutation of All Heresies*): *hodòs áno káto mía kaì skoliéi* – 'way up down one and the same' (Heraclitus, 1987, 40). Receiving news about his old classmates from the retired headmaster of Portora Royal School, Douglas Graham, Beckett repeats the oxymoronic version of

Figure 12 Beckett on the set of *Quadrat*, Stuttgart (1981).

Heraclitus's dictum that will govern 'The Way': 'Up & down the long crooked straight we potter somehow on and no words left to help' (Beckett, 2016, 680). This too seems a remembrance of Heraclitus, the axiom (also preserved in Hippolytus) equating writing with wayfaring: 'The way of writing (*graphéon hodòs*) is straight and crooked' (Heraclitus, 1987, 40).

'In unending ending' one file shuffles along a vertical figure eight, a second along a horizontal one, inscribing the emblem of infinity. Editor Dirk Van Hulle calls this infinite Pre-Socratic gress 'the brief translation of a philosophical metaphor and a way of thought' (Van Hulle, 2009, xiii). It is a way of putting thought through its paces, Beckett again attending closely to pace: 'Gait down as up same plodding always. A foot a second or mile an hour and more' (Beckett, 2009a, 125). The stark course is however no mathematical abstraction: Beckett establishes a barren terrain of loose sand and bedrock bordered by Golgotha thorns, effacing the tracks of previous pacers. Carlton Lake calls the piece 'the distillation of all the journeys made by all of Beckett's eternal wanderers' (Lake, 1984, 174).

The pedestrian liberty extolled since Rousseau is in 'The Way' a momentary respite: 'Briefly once at the extremes the will set free' (125); 'the same leisure once at either end to pause or not' (126). By situating anonymous wayfarers along a symbolic yet organic and mineral landscape, hemming it with vegetation (a second recursive process) and paving it with stone and sand, Beckett rescues from algebraic abstraction the walker's validation of social practices and forms of life, however minimal they may be. The walk subdues the will but does not suppress it. A contaminant in formal logic, the will is 'set free' fleetingly yet long enough for the wayfarer to disrupt the geometric glyph, an instant that the text too occupies long enough to articulate the character of its subjugation.

So Beckett does not so much dispel the walking myth in these late pieces as align it with cybernetic models of recursiveness that precede and exceed it. Recursion is a primary mechanism of reiteration: repetition, emulation and variation, inherent to the human body and syntax as to internal combustion engines, Russian dolls, orchestral fugues, tides, vegetation and myriad other phenomena; circuit moving within another without telos beyond the maintenance of homeostasis in changing environments. Molloy's sucking stones trace one, as do the manic combinatorics of *Watt*. In rhetorical as well as physical and psychological terms recursiveness is regression, literally 'walking back', including Molloy's walk back home to mother, Moran's attempt to retrace it, and the rondo of *How It Is*, *Come and Go*, *Quad* and 'The Way'. (The very manuscript of recursive *En attendant Godot* traces an epigraphic regression, the second act drafted back to front on the verso of the first act's recto.) These recursive walks are not a progress from question to answer, from complaint to cure, or from damnation to salvation. The *vient-et-va* is not a footloose amble into well-being but amble *as* being, on the way to being; a governing condition of possibility and limit, not so much without hope as beyond expectation.

Already while his ship berthed in Le Havre *en route* to Germany in 1936 Beckett wearily forecasted: 'Tired of walking around. But what will Germany be, for 6 ? months, but walking around, mainly?' (qtd in Nixon, 2011, 16). It mainly proved to be so. 'An oscillation is not solved by its coming to rest', Beckett lamented in a 1 March 1937 entry near the end of his *Bildungsreise* in Munich (qtd in Nixon, 2011, 191). Where the flâneur, a restless loiterer, recognises no such dichotomy, Beckett sought equipoise. Eventually it would arise from oscillation. Quando il piede cammina il cuore posa. 'Never once have I stopped', declares The Unnamable. 'My halts do not count. Their purpose was to enable me to go on' (Beckett, 1958a, 45). In its final formulation almost a half-century later: 'Stirrings Still'.

'Die Flucht vor dem erlösenden Ruhepunkt, dem Nichts, ist seinem [Becketts] Gehen immer gegenwärtig', writes Annelie Lütgens: The flight from the redemptive resting point, the nothing, is ever present in Beckett's walking (Lütgens, 2007, 32; my translation). Or as Jean-Michel Rabaté asserts: 'A Kantian imperative to "go on", but in style, and this despite all the odds, remains Beckett's enduring ethical testament' (Rabaté, 2015, 167–8). Yet already by the time of the composition of the trilogy, the Beckett walk can go on only by abjuring ethics and style: 'I've just crawled out, perhaps I went silent, no, I say that in order to say something, in order to go on a little more, you must go on a little more, you must go on a long time more, you must go on evermore' (Beckett, 1958a, 152).

'Pure and Mere Gress'

Employing gressive alternatives to purposive linear plotting, Beckett would devise the autotelic structures of his quietist late fiction. 'Stirrings Still' and the three stories of *Nohow On* share a primarily peripatetic organization, without extrinsic justification or narrative arc. In this Beckett anticipates such proponents of a non-teleological conception of being as the anti-Aristotelian philosophers Kieran Setiva and Frédéric Gros and the Buddhist monk Thich Nhat Hanh, who identify aimless walking as the exemplary non-purposive activity. For them, indeterminate walking promotes the dissolution of the ego and the reabsorption through distributed cognition into the immediacy and agency of the path. Where intent may narrow and cramp the mind, aimlessness diffuses it and induces acceptance. Gros writes that 'once you no longer expect anything from the world on these aimless and peaceful walks, that is when the world delivers itself to you, gives itself, yields itself up. When you no

Figure 13 First edition cover illustrated by Alberto Giacometti,
L'Homme qui marche (1951).

longer expect anything' (Gros, 2014, 79). Though without this post-Romantic
sense of plenitude, worlds are indeed yielded to Beckett's expectationless
walkers – in *Nohow On* charged worlds of guardians, occult voices and expressive objects. 'The old haunts were never more present,' Beckett writes to Eoin
O'Brien on 16 May 1985. 'With closed eyes I walk those back roads' (O'Brien,
1986, 352).

For Hanh, the unmotivated Zen walk 'simply means walking while being
aware of each step and of our breathing' (Hanh, 2015, 79). The protagonists of
Nohow On are intent only on their steps. In *Company* the 'old man plodding
along a narrow country road' counts his: 'Sole sound in the silence is your
footfall. Rather sole sounds for they vary from one to the next. You listen to each
one and add it in your mind to the growing sum of those that went before'
(Beckett, 1996, 9). The succession of steps is reason enough and future enough.
In Zen, mind evacuated and the feet aware, one walks quietly with one's dead;
'I walk for my father', Hanh attests, and with him towards nirvana (Hanh,
2015, 60). The son in Beckett's *Company* walks with his 'father's shade. In his
old tramping rags. Finally on side by side from nought anew' (Beckett, 1996, 9).
The widow's walk in *Ill Seen Ill Said* approaches the figment of her mourned
husband, recognizably in those same tramping rags: 'Dark greatcoat reaching to
the ground. Antiquated block hat' (60). *Worstward Ho* conjures a child's walk

between these parental shades towards Beckett's Schopenhauerian version of nirvana, 'evermost almost void' (113).

Beckett had been taking filial walks for almost a half century. 'Lovely walk this morning with Father', Beckett told Thomas MacGreevy on 23 April 1933. 'I'll never have anyone like him' (Beckett, 2009b, 154). That June William Beckett died of a heart attack. 'I can't write about him', Beckett wrote to MacGreevy on 2 July 1933, 'I can only walk the fields and climb the ditches after him' (165). And did so: 'I thought of a Xmas morning not long ago standing at the back of the Scalp with Father, hearing singing coming from the Glencullan Chapel', Beckett wrote to MacGreevy on New Year's Day 1935 (239). 'Melancholy memories of other Xmas walks', Beckett wrote in his diary after a long walk in the Berlin environs on Christmas 1936 (qtd in Nixon, 2011, 43). On 27 December 1954 he wrote to Pamela Mitchell after a walk near his chalet at Ussy, 'the real walk was elsewhere, on a screen inside' (qtd in Nixon, 2011, 43), while in a 21 May 1955 letter to Mary Manning Howe he made it clear that this 'real walk' was filial: 'At night, when I can't sleep, I do the old walks again and stand beside him again one Xmas morning in the fields near Glencullen, listening to chapel bells' (qtd in Nixon, 2011, 43).

Already in the early French fiction of 'La Fin' ('The End'), Beckett was resuming these filial walks. 'It was evening, I was with my father on a height, he held my hand. I would have liked him to draw me close with a gesture of protective love, but his mind was on other things. He also taught me the names of the mountains' (Beckett, 1995, 98–9). This father is an aloof guide and denominator, like the Archangel Gabriel instructing Adam on cosmology from a peak in *Paradise Lost*. In 'From an Abandoned Work' Beckett then fixes the allusion to Milton but reverses the preceptor's role: 'One day I told him about Milton's cosmology, away up in the mountains we were, resting against a huge rock looking out to sea, that impressed him hugely' (158).

In *Texts for Nothing* I the pair follows a level trail leading east of Eden: 'we walked together, hand in hand, silent, sunk in our worlds, each in his worlds, the hands forgotten in each other. That's how I've held out till now' (Beckett, 1995, 103–4). 'They hand in hand with wand'ring steps and slow/ Through Eden took thir solitary way' (Milton, 1952, 281): Beckett's pair adopts the manual gesture, slack meander, and shared solitude of Milton's expelled couple but, home forgotten and destination forsworn, without the prophesied restoration. The union of father and son occurs not at a location but along a direction.

In *Company* the son 'plodding along a narrow road' since dawn senses in the evening 'your father's shade' (Beckett, 1996, 9). He imaginatively reconstructs the father's 'tramp in the mountains' to evade his son's birth. Unlike the fleeing father of 'First Love' he duly returns to his family, and now his shade, still in tramping dress, escorts his aging son towards the void: 'Topcoat once green stiff with age and grime from chin to insteps. Battered once buff block hat and quarter boots still a match' (16). The pair proceeds afresh beyond all calculation and judgment: 'Reckoning ended on together from nought anew' (16).

Beckett told John Pilling in 1969 that writing *Molloy* 'was like taking a walk' (Pilling, 2015, 15), and *Nohow On* reads as one. The second trilogy (as well as 'Stirrings Still') has a pronounced peripatetic organization: each story is presented as a set of dim paths sketched out rather than mapped, a performance seemingly without itinerary. Typography and punctuation furnish prose equivalents to the pedestrian rhythm of 'mirlitonnades': 'pas à pas/ nulle part/ nul seul/ ne sait comment/ petits pas/ nulle part/ obstinément' (Beckett, 2012, 216). This is an emphysema pace – short of breath. Paragraphing is shrunk into compact discrete units of short phrases and punctuation reduced almost entirely to periods, beyond which Beckett retains only what audibly registers respiration: the dash, exclamation and question mark. 'To tell', Tim Ingold proposes, 'is not to represent the world but to trace a path through it that others can follow' (Ingold, 2011, 163), a conception of narration that overtly structures the second trilogy.

Company is yet another of Beckett's variations on 'stirrings still. Unformulable gropings of the mind. Unstillable' (16). This restlessness determines the doubling-back diegesis: an inverted doppelgänger tale where the doubles, a memorializing 'voice' and a fabulating 'devisor', are finally the banished figments of a disabled solitary. The paralytic son in his 'windowless' monad of a cell is reminded of filial and unaccompanied walks across a specifically Irish landscape, covering 'some twenty-five thousand leagues or roughly thrice the girdle. And never once overstepped a radius of one from home' (44 and 45). The dominant walk is a 'beeline' (line of being) across the pasture through the snow, steps no longer computed because 'they number each day the same. Average day in day out the same. The way being always the same' (26). The Heraclitian one-and-the-same road to being, as later in 'The Way'.

On his last walk he is becoming a figment, like *L'homme qui marche* and other walkers of Beckett's collaborator Alberto Giacometti (see Figure 13), for 'you do not hear your footfalls any more' (26). Nor can he sense his father any more, despite having donned his very attire to inhabit him. The restless walker who, as in 'The Way', halts only long enough to turn back is suddenly paralysed, as had been Beckett while in filial mourning. 'The bad years were between when I had to crawl home in 1932 and after my father's death in 1933', he told James Knowlson; 'I'll tell you how it was. I was walking down Dawson Street. And I felt I couldn't go on. It was a strange experience I can't really describe. I found I couldn't go on moving. So I went into the nearest pub and got a drink just to stay still' (Knowlson, 1996, 167). He entered psycho-analysis under Wilfred Bion at the Tavistock Clinic in 1933 reporting 'total paralysis' as the most severe symptom of his anxiety (169). In *Company* this ordeal is transposed onto an aberrant pedestrian geometry. He stares at his feet: 'Can they go on? Or better, Shall they go on?'

> You at a standstill in the midst. The quarter boots sunk to the tops. The skirts of the greatcoat resting on the snow. In the old bowed head in the old block hat speechless misgiving. Halfway across the pasture on your beeline to the gap. The unerring feet fast. You look behind you as you could not then and see their trail. A great swerve. Withershins. Almost as if all at once the heart too heavy. In the end too heavy. (Beckett, 1996, 27–8)

A counter-clockwise deviation from the line of being induces paralysis, but the onward fiat prevails. Narration elides motion and inscription: 'But to be going on with let him crawl' (34). 'With bootless crawl' he proceeds (40), punning footwear off Shakespeare's futile or "bootless cries" that "trouble deaf heaven" in Sonnet 29 (line 3, Shakespeare, 1986, 91), but notably the text too will crawl: 'Can the crawling creator crawling in the same create dark as his creature create while crawling?' (38) Even as the narrator then denies this tongue-twisting possibility the text affirms it, in the very formula of the filial walk: 'Then on from nought anew' (45).

In *Ill Seen Ill Said* a widow envisions among a dozen druidic guardians her dead husband, recognizably the tramping father of *Company*. Oriented around a black granite slab, her mourning routine inscribes the *aditus-transitus-abitus*: 'On her way out with the flowers as unerring as best she can she lingers by it. As on her way back with empty hands. Lingers by it a while on her way on' (Beckett, 1996, 75). The necromantic menhir exercises a preternatural agency: 'But when the stone draws then to her feet the prayer, Take her' (53). As in pilgrimage, Zen and other ascetic and apophatic regimens, the walk becomes the prayer.

Like May in *Footfalls*, the widow's tread is ethereal: 'Slowly with fluttering step as if wanting mass' (61). 'Her steps so light they barely leave a trace' (67) in the snowy pasture walked also in *Company*; 'little by little her footprints are effaced' (55). Yet when the narrative tries to negate the 'trace' of this 'inexist-ent' creature, she manages to leave footprints even while vanishing. 'And what if the eye could not? No more tear itself away from the remains of trace. Of what was never. Quick say it suddenly can and farewell say say farewell. If only to the face. Of her tenacious trace' (86). To the '*tenace trace*' of the original French (Beckett, 1981, 75) inheres the sense of 'trail' or 'spoor' that the English carries. Even as the erratic syntax struggles to efface it, the narrative eye cannot help but follow this indelible trace that is equally a trail, footprints, and the lines on the page – contiguously ground, body and text.

All of the stories of the triptych reproduce syntactically and lexically the enfeebled tread. Meandering narration warily undergoes revision, retraction, cancellation, pauses and editorial asides. The text of *Ill Seen Ill Said* potters in step with its slow uncertain widow: 'Gently gently. On. Careful' (58). The rhythm of *Worstward Ho* follows the track of the trudging pair: 'Left right left right barefoot unreceding on. They then the words' (Beckett, 1996, 105). An immobile creator devises a pedestrian tableau vivant in a saccadic language that strives to coincide with the pedestrian image conjured, one that finally ebbs from representation. The terse, monosyllabic phrases lumber along, textuality proceeding under the impress of gression. Without destination the text walks barefoot on his beloved Keats's 'naked foot of Poesy' (Keats, 1956, 371).

The intentions that give rise to the walk diminish once the walker sets out, as Tim Ingold notes: 'he and his walking become one and the same. And while there is of course a mind at work in the attentionality of *walking*, just as there is in the intentionality of *going for a walk*, this is a mind immanent in the movement itself rather than an originating source to which such movement may be attributed as an effect' (Ingold, 2015, 133). *Worstward Ho* presents a mind immanent in movement, origin reduced to filial relation and the parental blazon of signature 'tramping rags'. As narration itself is explicitly in movement, the authorial mind too becomes immanent.

In the characteristic walking poem adapted from Romanticism, the walk naturalises literary procedures, Wordsworth and Coleridge composing *Lyrical Ballads* afoot and extempore. In 'The Woodpile', for instance, Robert Frost happens upon his own insight; experience is heightened and contemplation enlarged without disruption of a rural routine. In the succession of expository details and mimetic informality, the poem's language assimilates itself to the peripatetic situation of the utterance (see Gilbert, 1991, 23–6). Beckett likewise manipulates the phatic and rhythmic possibilities, but unlike Frost's his are walks not of observation but of immersion and participation, and he exposes the representational hiatus between perambulatory and textual operations. Beckett renders overt the hindered advance of composition within a recalcitrant literary medium. The walk undergoes cycles of revision and even recantation, yet also of stubborn recursion: 'plod on from nought anew' (Beckett, 1996, 27).

Worstward Ho painstakingly assembles then surrenders a walking image of tender abidance in a panting yet dogged language, rhetorically breathless. The imaginative recourse to filial path-following becomes a key to moral persistence. With 'the hand forgotten in each other', Beckett devises his happiest image, and with it replenishes his late style. Beckett constructs a provisional tableau vivant not in spite but by means of the instability of language and the erosion of faculties:

> Hand in hand with equal plod they go. In the free hands – no. Free empty hands. Backs turned both bowed with equal plod they go. The child hand raised to reach the holding hand. Hold the old holding hand. Hold and be held. Plod on and never recede. Slowly and with never a pause plod on and never recede. Backs turned. Both bowed. Joined by held holding hands. Plod on as one. One shade. Another shade. (Beckett, 1996, 93)

Again the matching Miltonic step into mortal adhesion: 'The as one plodding train' (98). Like the disintegrating limbs of Giacometti's charcoal walker illustrating the first American edition of the story, Beckett's language steps towards its own dissolution, and in defiance of it.

A description of footwear is retracted: 'The boots. Better worse bootless. Bare heels' (100). The again punning stress on barefootedness suggests not abstraction into an idealised space or destitution but elemental adamic contact with the ground, a way of knowing. Gerard Manley Hopkins, buried near William Beckett's grave outside Dublin, in 'God's Grandeur' descries numbing footwear: 'nor can foot feel, being shod' (Hopkins, 1970, 66). The skin-deep thinking of the sole is usually beneath consideration on the contemptible obverse surface of the hard-shod feet, but Beckett returns attention to that surface, to the foot's knowledge. Reduced even to 'pins' in 'dimmost dim', the limbs feel their way to the 'bounds of boundless void' (Beckett, 1996, 116). (The barefoot ghost of the father had already appeared to Watt, indeed was more stable to him than the incident of the Galls: 'the time when his dead father appeared to him in a wood, with his trousers rolled up over his knees and his shoes and socks in his hand'; Beckett, 2009c, 60).

Barefoot and back turned they walk out on social station, background, personhood; even domestic nomenclature is generalised into seniority ('an old man and child', an 'old woman'; Beckett, 1996, 93 and 113). 'By walking, you can escape from the very idea of identity, the temptation to be someone, to have a name and a history', writes Gros. 'The freedom of walking lies in not being anyone; for the walking body has no history, it is just an eddy in the stream of immemorial life' (Gros, 2014, 6–7). The tendency of *Worstward Ho* is to anonymise and relieve of historicity the walking body, which otherwise belongs firmly to social as well as physical mobility. The intransitive onwardness minimises aspiration and so forecloses the sense of historical purpose.

The hortatory striving of the Victorian progressive had already been chastened in the culminating contradiction of *The Unnamable*: 'I can't go on, I'll go on' (Beckett, 1958a, 79). 'So on', states the terminal 'Stirrings Still': 'Was he then now to press on regardless now in one direction and now in another' (Beckett, 1995, 264). In 'Rugby Chapel', Matthew Arnold's journeying father Thomas, who had introduced his son to Wordsworth, hectors the wanderers to 'strengthen the wavering line,/ Stablish, continue our march,/ On, to the bound of the waste,/ On, to the city of God' (ll. 205–8; Arnold, 1883, 263). On to the bound of the waste – 'bounds of boundless void' – is the impetus of *Worstward Ho*, but this father is mercifully silent: 'somehow on to the dim. The void. The shades' (Beckett, 1996, 110). Where Arnold in 'The Scholar Gypsy' exhorts one to a morally exemplary aimless-ness, Beckett censors oratory and plays *on* against its negating palindrome *no*: 'On. Say on. Be said on. Somehow on. Till nohow on' (89). In an unpublished poem drafted on the manuscript of *Worstward Ho*, Beckett jingles: 'on whence/ no sense/ but on/ to whence/ no sense' (Beckett, 2012, 470). In French he plays the step of *pas* against its negating homonym *pas*. He translated *Footfalls* as *Pas*, which culminates in pacing May's perverse denial 'je n'étais pas là' (Beckett, 1978, 16).

'Said nohow on' (Beckett, 1996, 116): the last two words of this 'second trilogy' course back to its first two words, *Nohow On*, Beckett's title for the collection that *Worstward Ho* completes. What is 'said' in this da capo structure proves a recursive formula, the homophonic knowhow to proceed and nohow to proceed there, a process that nevertheless goes 'on' in oscilla-tion between these charged poles of affirmation and negation. This is not a senseless scurry, for the shuttle is not merely reported but also illocutionary, both something 'said' and something done – 'on'. The dynamism of this performative pedestrian enunciation affronts the 'unworseable evermost almost void' it would denominate and exorcise: 'Less worse then? Enough. A pox on void' (113).

On in Beckett is a prepositional imperative governing writing and reading as well as walking. It is a term of spatial contiguity, an instruction to cover the ground and cover the page. Beckett summarised his artistic imperative to Juliet in a pedestrian cliché: every new work must be '"un pas en avant"', a step forward (qtd in Juliet, 1986, 17). In the word *on* converges this bipedal and manual imprint. In *Worstward Ho*, the homology between walking and writing turns existential: 'On. Stare on. Say on. Be on. Somehow on' (Beckett, 1996, 101). Directing the 1967 West Berlin production of *Endspiel*, Beckett cautioned his Schiller-Theater players against Heideggerian notions of becoming. 'Ein Werden kann es nicht geben. Nur ein Weitermachen. Die Formel dafür ist "Spiel"': 'There cannot be a becoming. Only a going on. The formula for this is "Play"' (qtd in Van Hulle and Weller, 2017, 209). Play extends from the dramatic action to the theatre itself and to composition. *Weitermachen* dissolves the existentialist dichotomy of becoming and being; *on* towards inaccessible being without the organicist metaphors of growth. Not becoming but coming-biding-going, the circuit Clov is trying to complete at the end of *Endgame*.

The *on* in Beckett's pedestrian ontology is active both still and stirring. 'At rest plodding on' in *Worstward Ho* because deeply at rest *while* plodding on (Beckett, 1996, 94). This is the treadmilling *'piétinement sur place'* Beckett described in Racine during his early Trinity College lectures (Knowlson and Knowlson, 2006, 312). In his last story it is the oxymoronic 'stirrings still': 'From where he sat he watched himself rise and go' (Beckett, 1995, 260). Each step of compulsive locomotion recalled by the paralytic in *Company* contains a fleeting moment of immobility: the 'sole' on which he puns 'cleaves to the ground bringing the body to a stand' (Beckett, 1996, 27). In *Ill Seen Ill Said* the itinerary is without origin or end: 'She still without stopping. On her way without starting. Gone without going. Back without returning' (58). This oscillation is anticipated by Clov on the threshold of departure, the journey so internalised that setting off seems superfluous.

In wayfaring, writes Ingold, 'things are instantiated in the world as their paths of movement, not as objects located in space. They *are* their stories. Here it is the movement itself that counts, not the destinations it connects' (Ingold, 2011, 162). He distinguishes it from plotted navigation to argue that 'it is through wayfaring and not transmission that knowledge is carried on' (143):

> the navigator has before him a complete representation of the territory, in the form of a cartographic map, upon which he can plot a course even before setting out. The journey then is no more than an explication of the plot. In wayfaring, by contrast, one follows a path that one has previously travelled in the company of others, or in their footsteps, reconstructing the itinerary as one goes along. (Ingold, 2007, 15–16)

This kind of wayfaring increasingly dominates *Nohow On*, in which mourners follow the path of a husband and father, and narrative is reconstructed every step of the way. This is not however a Grail quest, for whereas navigation is ends-directed, wayfaring recognises only stations in a relay.

Ingold approximates the Beckettian trajectory of *aditus-transitus-abitus*: 'The path of the wayfarer wends hither and thither, and may even pause here and there before moving on. But it has no beginning or end. While on the trail the wayfarer is always somewhere, yet every "somewhere" is on the way to somewhere else. The inhabited world is a reticulated meshwork of such trails, which is continually being woven as life goes on along them' (Ingold, 2007, 81). Beckett's characters and his texts move along rather than across a terrain, the path instantiating both.

It is 'by *going around* in an environment', Ingold affirms, that people come to know, and this knowledge 'is integrated not *up* the levels of a classification but *along* paths of movement, and people grow into it by following trails through a meshwork' (Ingold, 2011, 143; see also Ingold, 2007, 91). Walking is the means by which stories are converted to a form of knowledge that is enmeshed in vital forces rather than issuing in hypostatised forms: 'knowledge is not classificatory. It is rather *storied*' (Ingold, 2011, 159). 'The storied world' is one 'of movement and becoming, in which any thing – caught at a particular place and moment – enfolds within its constitution the history of relations that have brought it there. In such a world, we can understand the nature of things only by attending to their relations, or in other words, by telling their stories' (160). Drawing on de Certeau and on the mechanics of the ductus in handwriting, Ingold equates walk and text: 'Every text, story or trip, in short, is a journey made rather than an object found' (Ingold, 2007, 16).

The shuffling, digressive stravagers of Beckett's stories deviate from the swift, efficient navigation of the prudent goal-oriented striver after social rewards who is parodied in 'Act without Words II'. Like Ingold's wayfarer they move along a graded ground rather than across the levelled vectors of the high-speed passenger. This is a ground not of point-to-point connection but 'threads and traces' (Ingold, 2007, 103) – a vocabulary recalling Beckett's definition of the aesthetic as '*traces profondes*' (Beckett, 1983, 152). As traces on the page, the walk is subject ceaselessly to impression and effacement. Consciousness cannot contain faithfully the filial walk, memory cannot retrieve its details impartially, and language cannot order it definitively. Yet, even as the late texts underscore the representational limitations of conflating pedestrian and textual operations, Beckett's hither-here-hence dynamic ever more emphatically associates them. While language in Beckett is scored by the force of the void it would affront, such erosion is a paradoxical condition of the prose's vitality. Phonemes collide to form novel conjunctions, no sooner compounded than atomised; statements are rescinded and images dimmed but, as it was for the Dadaists, destruction is his Beatrice. There is in this refusal of hope a moral as well as aesthetic tenacity, at least in the terms of Wittgenstein's equation in the *Tractatus*, a book he annotated and kept in his library (see Van Hulle and Nixon, 2013, 163–7 and 249–51): 'Ethik und Ästhetik sind eins' – 'Ethics and aesthetics are one' (*Tractatus* 6.421; Wittgenstein, 1984, 83). According to Wittgenstein, the work of art may manifest what is otherwise ineffable. Ethics, recalcitrant to discursive determination, is not simply illustrated in the work of art but, operating at the limits of the sayable, the work may itself constitute an ethics (see Furlani, 2015, 63–8).

In his copy of *Der Namenlose*, Elmar Tophoven's translation of *The Unnamable*, Theodor Adorno, detecting as in other places a perceived influence of Wittgenstein on Beckett, underlined two appearances of the verb *weitermachen* (go on), noting in the margin: 'Going on is a major category. And a *critical* one: against the deception of the question of meaning' (Adorno, 1994, 56). As Shane Weller observes in quoting this marginalia, Adorno locates in Beckett an exemplary ethical commitment to going on in the absence of an absolute negativity. Weller writes that 'Beckett's writing of the negative in *The Unnamable* is in fact a writing of the *failure* of the negative, but a failure that never results in the abandonment of the task at hand' (Weller, 2010, 192). Beckett's aesthetic insistence 'on the need to "go on"' is, he argues, ethical in Adorno's sense (193); as certainly in Wittgenstein's.

Trekking the Beckettian *spookwegen* of *The Old Ways*, Robert Macfarlane understands 'walking as enabling sight and thought rather than encouraging retreat and escape; paths as offering not only means of traversing space, but also ways of feeling, being and knowing' (Macfarlane, 2012, 24). He asserts that 'walking is not the action by which one arrives at knowledge; it is itself the means of knowing' (27). This is the only kind of knowledge that in Beckett receives any validation: knowledge through the body along the way, ultimately a resigned knowledge. *The Unnamable* advises that 'all that is needed is to wander and let wander, be this slow boundless whirlwind and every particle of its dust, it's impossible' (Beckett, 1958a, 161).

Maude observes that in Beckett 'the habitual and the automatic become progressively more central, until in the late works, habit and mechanical behaviour constitute a tenuous, fraught and primitive ontology, the residues of an agential self' (Maude, 2015, 183). The walk, Beckett's paradigmatic act of habit and mechanical behaviour, proves peculiarly regenerative and creative, imprinted the length of his wayfaring works and days from those formative hikes with his father to their final instantiation in *Worstward Ho*. 'Nohow nought, nohow on': Beckett's *via negativa* is decidedly a *via pedestrem*, a footpath of unknowing, indigence, and privation of the epistemic armature that purposive, goal-oriented navigation presumes (Beckett, 1996, 116). The aimless lope becomes an apophatic emblem, at the limit of possibility and beyond all anodyne meaning, of ongoing approach to unnameable being.

Works Cited

Abrams, M. H. (1970), 'Structure and Style in the Greater Romantic Lyric', in Harold Bloom (ed.), *Romanticism and Consciousness*, New York: Norton, pp. 201–32.

Abrams, M. H. (1971), *Natural Supernaturalism*, New York: Norton.

Ackerley, C. J. (2012), 'Monadology: Samuel Beckett and Gottfried Wilhelm Leibniz', in Matthew Feldman and Karim Mamdani (eds), *Beckett/Philosophy*, Sophia: University Press of St. Kliment Ohridski, pp. 140–61.

Ackerley, C. J. and S. E. Gontarski (2004), *The Grove Companion to Samuel Beckett*, New York: Grove Press.

Adorno, Theodor W. (1994), *Frankfurter Adorno Blätter III*, ed. Theodor W. Adorno Archiv, Munich: edition text + kritik.

Amato, Joseph, A. (2004), *On Foot: A History of Walking*, New York: New York University Press.

Aragon, Louis (1972), *Le paysan de Paris*, Paris: Gallimard.

Aragon, Louis (1994), *Paris Peasant*, trans. Simon Watson Taylor, Boston: Exact Change.

Arnold, Matthew (1883), *Poems*, second volume, New York: Macmillan and Co.

Asmus, Walter D. (1979), 'Im Theater-Alltag tut man sich schwerer: Beckett inszeniert *Warten auf Godot*', in Hartmut Engelhardt and Dieter Mettler (eds), *Materialien zu Samuel Becketts 'Warten auf Godot'*, Band 2, Frankfurt: Suhrkamp Verlag, pp. 312–24.

Balzac, Honoré de (2016), 'Théorie de la démarche', in Thierry Paquot and Frédéric Rossi (eds), *Flâner à Paris: Petite anthologie littéraire du XIXe siècle*. Gollion: Infolio éditions, pp. 37–94.

Beckett, Samuel (1951), *Malone muert*, Paris: Editions de Minuit.

Beckett, Samuel (1953), *L'Innommable*, Paris: Editions de Minuit.

Beckett, Samuel (1955), *Molloy*, trans. Patrick Bowles, in collaboration with the author, New York: Grove Press.

Beckett, Samuel (1956), *Malone Dies*, New York: Grove Weidenfeld.

Beckett, Samuel (1957), *Fin de partie*, Paris: Editions de Minuit.

Beckett, Samuel (1958a), *The Unnamable*, New York: Grove Press.

Beckett, Samuel (1958b), *Nouvelles et Textes pour rien*, Paris: Editions de Minuit.

Beckett, Samuel (1958c), *Endgame* and *Act without Words*, New York: Grove Press.

Beckett, Samuel (1961), *Comment c'est*, Paris: Editions de Minuit.

Beckett, Samuel (1964), *How It Is*, New York: Grove Press.

Beckett, Samuel (1970a), *Mercier et Camier*, Paris: Editions de Minuit.

Beckett, Samuel (1970b), *Murphy*, New York: Grove Press.

Beckett, Samuel (1970c), *Premier amour*, Paris: Editions de Minuit.

Beckett, Samuel (1971), *En attendant Godot. Théâtre I*, Paris: Editions de Minuit.

Beckett, Samuel (1974), *More Pricks than Kicks*, London: Picador.

Beckett, Samuel (1976), *Pour finir encore et autres foirades*, Paris: Editions de Minuit.

Beckett, Samuel (1978), *Poèmes suivi de mirlitonnades*, Paris: Editions de Minuit.

Beckett, Samuel (1981), *Mal vu mal dit*, Paris: Editions de Minuit.

Beckett, Samuel (1982a), *Molloy*, Paris: Editions de Minuit.

Beckett, Samuel (1982b), *Waiting for Godot*, New York: Grove Press.

Beckett, Samuel (1983), *Disjecta: Miscellaneous Writings and a Dramatic Fragment*, ed. Ruby Cohn, London: John Calder.

Beckett, Samuel (1984), *The Collected Shorter Plays of Samuel Beckett*, New York: Grove Weidenfeld.

Beckett, Samuel (1986), *Catastrophe et autres dramaticules*, Paris: Editions de Minuit.

Beckett, Samuel (1988), *Mercier and Camier*, London: Picador.

Beckett, Samuel (1993), *Dream of Fair to Middling Women*, ed. Eoin O' Brien and Edith Fournier, London: Calder.

Beckett, Samuel (1995), *The Complete Short Prose, 1929–1989*, ed. Stanley E. Gontarski, New York: Grove Press.

Beckett, Samuel (1996), *Nohow On*, New York: Grove Press.

Beckett, Samuel (1999), *Beckett's 'Dream' Notebook*, ed. John Pilling, Reading: Beckett International Foundation.

Beckett, Samuel (2009a), *Company, Ill Seen Ill Said, Worstward Ho, Stirring Still*, ed. Dirk Van Hulle, London: Faber and Faber.

Beckett, Samuel (2009b), *The Letters of Samuel Beckett, Vol. I: 1929–1940*, ed. Martha Dow Fehsenfeld and Lois More Overbeck, Cambridge: Cambridge University Press.

Beckett, Samuel (2009c), *Watt*, ed. C. J. Ackerley, London: Faber and Faber.

Beckett, Samuel (2011), *The Letters of Samuel Beckett, Volume II: 1941–1956*, ed. George Craig, Martha Dow Fehsenfeld, Dan Gunn and Lois More Overbeck, Cambridge: Cambridge University Press.

Beckett, Samuel (2012), *The Collected Poems of Samuel Beckett*, ed. Seán Lawlor and John Pilling, London: Faber and Faber.

Beckett, Samuel (2014a), *Echo's Bones*, ed. Mark Nixon, London: Faber and Faber.

Beckett, Samuel (2014b), *The Letters of Samuel Beckett, Vol. III: 1957–1965*, ed. George Craig, Martha Dow Fehsenfeld, Dan Gunn and Lois More Overbeck, Cambridge: Cambridge University Press.

Beckett, Samuel (2016), *The Letters of Samuel Beckett, Volume IV: 1966–1989*, ed. George Craig, Martha Dow Fehsenfeld, Dan Gunn and Lois More Overbeck, Cambridge: Cambridge University Press.

Beckett, Samuel (2020), *Samuel Beckett's 'Philosophy Notes'*, ed. Stephen Matthews and Matthew Feldman with David Addyman, Oxford: Oxford University Press.

Beckett, Samuel *Sottisier* Notebook, UoR MS2460, Beckett International Foundation, The University of Reading.

Beckett, Samuel *Whoroscope* Notebook, UoR MS3000, Beckett International Foundation, The University of Reading.

Beckett, Samuel and Alan Schneider (1998), *No Author Better Served: The Correspondence of Samuel Beckett and Alan Schneider*, ed. Maurice Harmon, Cambridge, MA: Harvard University Press.

Belloc, Hilaire (1906), *Hills and the Sea*, London: Methuen.

Beloborodova, Olga (2020), *Postcognitivist Beckett*, Cambridge: Cambridge University Press.

Benjamin, Walter (1974), *Gesammelte Schriften 1.2*, ed. Rolf Tiedemann and Hermann Schweppenhäuser, Frankfurt: Suhrkamp Verlag.

Benjamin, Walter (1988), *Angelus Novus: Ausgewählte Schriften 2*, Frankfurt: Suhrkamp Verlag.

Benjamin, Walter (1999), *Arcades Project*, trans. Howard Eiland and Kevin McLauchlin, Cambridge, MA: Belknap Press.

Bennett, Jane (2010), *Vibrant Matter: A Political Ecology of Things*, Durham, NC: Duke University Press.

Bernhard, Thomas (1971), *Gehen*, Frankfurt: Suhrkamp.

Bloom, Harold (1970), 'The Internalization of the Quest Romance', in Harold Bloom (ed.), *Romanticism and Consciousness*, New York: Norton, pp. 3–23.

Breuer, Josef and Sigmund Freud (1955), *Studies on Hysteria*, ed. and trans. James Strachey, London: Hogarth Press.

Browne, Thomas (1896), *Hydrotaphia and The Garden of Cyrus*, ed. W. A. Greenhill, London: Macmillan and Co.

Bunyan, John (1987), *Pilgrim's Progress*, ed. Roger Sharrock, London: Penguin Books.

Burton, Robert (2001), *The Anatomy of Melancholy*, ed. Holbrook Jackson, New York: New York Review Books.

Burroughs, John (1896), *Winter Sunshine*, Edinburgh: David Douglas.

Byron, George Gordon (1967), *Childe Harold's Pilgrimage*, in *Selected Poetry of Lord Byron*, ed. Leslie A. Marchand, New York: Random House, pp. 3–170.

Cavendish, Margaret (2000), *Paper Bodies: A Margaret Cavendish Reader*, ed. Sylvia Bowerbank and Sara Mendelson, Peterborough: Broadview Press.

Certeau, Michel de (1988), *The Practice of Everyday Life*, trans. Steven Rendell, Berkeley: University of California Press.

Clark, Andy (2010), 'Coupling, Constitution, and the Cognitive Kind', in Richard Menary (ed.), *The Extended Mind*, Cambridge, MA: MIT Press, pp. 81–99.

Clark, Andy and David J. Chalmers (2010), 'The Extended Mind', in Richard Menary (ed.), *The Extended Mind*, Cambridge, MA: MIT Press, pp. 27–42.

Cohn, Ruby (2006), 'Ruby Cohn on the Godot Circle', in James Knowlson and Elizabeth Knowlson (eds), *Beckett Remembering / Remembering Beckett*, London: Bloomsbury, pp. 125–34.

Coleridge, Samuel Taylor (1907), *Biographia Literaria*, ed. John Shawcross, Oxford: Oxford University Press.

Coleridge, Samuel Taylor (1951), *Selected Poetry and Prose of Coleridge*, ed. Donald A. Stauffer, New York: Modern Library, pp. 78–82.

Cordingley, Anthony (2018), *Samuel Beckett's* How It Is: *Philosophy in Translation*, Edinburgh: University of Edinburgh Press.

Coverley, Merlin (2012), *The Art of Wandering: The Writer as Walker*, Harpenden: Oldcastle Books.

Davies, William Henry (1926), *The Autobiography of a Supertramp*, London: Jonathan Cape.

Dickens, Charles (1924), *The Old Curiosity Shop*, London: Chapman & Hall.

Dickens, Charles (2000), *The Uncommercial Traveller and Other Papers 1859–1870*, ed. Michael Slater and John Drew, London: J. M. Dent.

Freud, Sigmund (1959), *Beyond the Pleasure Principle*, trans. James Strachey, New York: Bantam Books.

Freud, Sigmund (1970), 'Das Unheimliche', in *Psychologische Schriften*, Studienausgabe Band IV, Frankfurt: S. Fischer Verlag, pp. 241–74.

Friedman, Alan Warren (2019), *Surreal Beckett: Samuel Beckett, James Joyce, and Surrealism*, New York: Routledge.

Frye, Northrop (1963), 'The Drunken Boat: The Revolutionary Element in Romanticism', in Northrop Frye (ed.), *Romanticism Reconsidered*, New York: Columbia University Press, pp. 1–25.

Furlani, Andre (2015), *Beckett after Wittgenstein*, Evanston, IL: Northwestern University Press.

Geulincx, Arnold (2006), *Ethics: with Samuel Beckett's Notes*, ed. Hans van Ruler, Anthony Uhlmann and Martin Wilson, trans. Martin Wilson, Leiden and Boston: Brill.

Gilbert, Roger (1991), *Walks in the World*, Princeton: Princeton University Press.

Goethe, Johann Wolfgang von (1986), *Goethes Werke,* Band III: *Dramatische Dichtungen* I, ed. Erik Trunz, Munich: Verlag C. H. Beck.

Gontarski, S. E. (1977), *Beckett's 'Happy Days':* A Manuscript Study, Columbus: Ohio State University Libraries Publications.

Gros, Frédéric (2014), *A Philosophy of Walking*, trans. John Howe, London: Verso.

Hacking, Ian (1998), *Mad Travelers: Reflections on the Reality of Transient Mental Illnesses*, Charlottesville, VA.: University Press of Virginia.

Hanh, Thich Nhat (2015), *How to Walk*, Berkeley, CA: Parallax Press.

Hartel, Gaby (2005), '"No stone unturned": Samuel Beckett sucht und findet ästhetische Anregungen im frühen deutschen Film', in Therese Fischer-Seidel and Marion Fries Dieckmann (eds), *Der unbekannte Beckett: Samuel Beckett und die deutsche Kultur*, Frankfurt: Suhrkamp, pp. 298–318.

Hartel, Gaby (2006), 'Ein großer Fußgänger': Samuel Beckett ist viel gewandert – auch in Berlin', in Lutz Dittrich, Carola Veit and Ernest Wichner (eds), *'Obergeschoss still closed': Samuel Beckett in Berlin 1936/37*, Berlin: Verlag Matthes und Seitz, pp. 13–26.

Hazlitt, William (1970), *Selected Writings*, ed. Ronald Blythe, London: Penguin.

Heraclitus. *Heraclitus* (1987), ed. and trans. Thomas M. Robinson, Toronto: University of Toronto Press.

Hessel, Franz (2012), *Spazieren in Berlin*, Berlin: Verlag für Berlin-Brandenburg.

Hölderlin, Friedrich (1963), 'Entwurf (Das älteste Systemprogramm des deutschen Idealismus)'. *Werke Briefe Dokumente*, ed. Friedrich Beißner, Munich: Winkler-Verlag, pp. 556–8.

Holmes, Oliver Wendell (1883), 'The Physiology of Walking', in *Pages from an Old Volume of Life: A Collection of Essays 1857–1881*, Boston: Houghton, Mifflin and Co., pp. 121–31.

Hopkins, Gerard Manley (1970), *The Poems of Gerard Manley Hopkins*, 4th ed., rev. and enlarged, ed. W. H. Gardner and W. N. MacKenzie, Oxford: Oxford University Press.

Hudson, W. H. (1982), *Afoot in England*, Oxford: Oxford University Press.

Ingold, Tim (2007), *Lines: A Short History*, London: Routledge.

Ingold, Tim (2011), *Being Alive: Essays on Movement, Knowledge and Description*, London: Routledge.

Ingold, Tim (2015), *The Life of Lines*, New York: Routledge.

Jarvis, Robin (1997), *Romantic Poetry and Pedestrian Travel*, London: Macmillan.

Juliet, Charles (1986), *Rencontres avec Samuel Beckett*, Paris: Editions Fata Morgana.

Kaspar, Frank (2007), 'Beckett Is Listening. Herbst 1963: Hamburger O-Töne und früh Radiowahrnehmung', in Michaela Giesing, Gaby Hartel and

Carol Veit (eds), *Das Raubauge in der Stadt: Beckett liest Hamburg*, Göttingen: Wallstein Verlag, pp. 60–78.

Keats, John (1956), *Poetical Works*, ed. Heathcote. W. Garrod, Oxford: Oxford University Press.

Kedzierski, Marek (2011), 'Barbara Bray in Her Own Words', *Modernism/Modernity*, 18:4, pp. 887–97.

Knabb, Ken, ed. and trans. (2006), *Situationist International Anthology*, Berkeley: Bureau of Public Secrets.

Knowlson, James (1996), *Damned to Fame: The Life of Samuel Beckett*, New York: Simon and Schuster.

Knowlson, James and Elizabeth Knowlson, eds. (2006), *Beckett Remembering / Remembering Beckett*, London: Bloomsbury.

Lake, Carlton (1984), *No Symbols Where None Intended*, Austin: Humanities Research Center, University of Texas at Austin.

Latour, Bruno (2004), *Politics of Nature: How to Bring the Sciences into Democracy*, trans. Catherine Porter, Cambridge, MA: Harvard University Press.

Leopardi, Giacomo (1998), *Canti*, ed. Franco Gavazzeni and Maria Maddalena Lobardi, Milano: Biblioteca Universale Rizzoli.

Lock, Charles (2024), 'Words on the Beach: Riddles of the Unpainted Shore and the Wrapped Coast', in Carsten Meiner and Katrine Helen Andersen (eds), *The Literary Beach: History and Aesthetics of a Modern Topos*, New York: Routledge, pp. 119–35.

Lütgens, Annelie (2007), 'Wohin gehen, wie gehen, warum gehen: Beckett und andere Künstler des Gehens im 20. Jahrhundert', in Michaela Giesing, Gaby Hartel and Carol Veit (eds), *Das Raubauge in der Stadt: Beckett liest Hamburg*, Göttingen: Wallstein Verlag, pp. 19–32.

Macfarlane, Robert (2012), *The Old Ways*, London: Penguin.

Mandelstam, Osip (2004), *The Selected Poems of Osip Mandelstam*, trans. Clarence Brown and William. S. Merwin, New York: New York Review Books.

Maude, Ulrike (2013), 'Somnambulism, Amnesia and Fugue: Beckett and (Male) Hysteria', in Peter Fifield and David Addyman (eds), *Samuel Beckett: Debts and Legacies*, London: Bloomsbury, pp. 153–76.

Maude, Ulrike (2015), 'Beckett, Body and Mind', in Dirk Van Hulle (ed.), *The New Cambridge Companion to Samuel Beckett*, Cambridge: Cambridge University Press, pp. 170–84.

Mayer, Andreas (2020), *The Science of Walking: Investigations into Locomotion in the Long Nineteenth Century*, rev. trans. Robin Blanton and Tilman Skowroneck, Chicago: University of Chicago Press.

Menary, Richard, ed. (2010), *The Extended Mind*, Cambridge, MA: MIT Press.

Meredith, George (1968), *The Egoist*, ed. George Woodcock, London: Penguin.

Merrifield, Andy (2005), *Guy Debord*, London: Reaktion.

Milton, John (1952), *Poetical Works of John Milton*, volume 1, ed. Helen Derbishire, Oxford: Oxford University Press.

Milton, John (1980), *The Complete Poems*, ed. Gordon Campbell, London: J. M. Dent and Sons.

Moor, Robert (2016), *On Trails*, New York: Simon and Schuster.

Nietzsche, Friedrich (1930), *Also Sprach Zarathustra*, Leipzig: Alfred Kröner Verlag.

Nixon, Mark (2006), '"the remains of trace": Intra- and Intertextual Transferences in Beckett's mirlitonnades Manuscripts', *Journal of Beckett Studies*, 16.1–2, pp. 96–122.

Nixon, Mark (2007), 'Beckett and Romanticism', *Samuel Beckett Today/ Aujourd'hui*, 18, pp. 61–76.

Nixon, Mark (2011), *Samuel Beckett's German Diaries, 1936–1937*, London: Continuum.

Nixon, Mark and Dirk Van Hulle (2017), *German Fever. Beckett in Deutschland. Marbacher Magazine* 158/159, Deutsches Literaturarchiv Marbach: Marbach am Neckar.

Noë, Alva (2009), *Out of Our Heads*, New York: Hill and Wang.

O'Brien, Eoin (1986), *The Beckett Country*, Dublin: Black Cat Press.

O'Mara, Shane (2019), *In Praise of Walking*, London: Bodley Head.

O'Reilly, Édouard Magessa, Dirk Van Hulle and Pim Verhulst (2017), *The Making of Samuel Beckett's 'Molloy'*, London: Bloomsbury.

Pilling, John (2015), 'Early Beckett: "The One Looking Through His Fingers"', in Dirk Van Hulle (ed.), *The New Cambridge Companion to Samuel Beckett*, Cambridge: Cambridge University Press, pp. 3–18.

Puttenham, George (2007), *The Art of English Poesy*, ed. Frank Whigham and Wayne A. Rebhorn, Ithaca, NY: Cornell University Press.

Rabaté, Jean-Michel (2015), 'Love and Lobsters: Beckett's Meta-Ethics', in Dirk Van Hulle (ed.), *The New Cambridge Companion to Samuel Beckett*, Cambridge: Cambridge University Press, pp. 158–69.

Rabinovitz, Rubin (1979), '*Molloy* and the Archetypal Traveller', *Journal of Beckett Studies*, 5, pp. 23–44.

Robinson, Jeffrey (2006), *The Walk: Notes on a Romantic Image*, London: Dalkey Archive.

Rousseau, Jean-Jacques (1953), *The Confessions*, trans. John. M. Cohen, London: Penguin.

Rousseau, Jean-Jacques (1997), *Les Rêveries du promeneur solitaire*, ed. Erik Leborgne, Paris: GF Flammarion.

Schopenhauer, Arthur (2010), *The World as Will and Representation*, volume I, trans. Judith Norman, Alistair Welchman and Christopher Janaway, Cambridge: Cambridge University Press.

Sebald, Winfried G. (2012), *"Auf ungeheuer dünnem Eis": Gespräche 1971 bis 2001*, ed. Torsten H. Hoffmann, Frankfurt: S. Fischer Verlag.

Shakespeare, William (1959), *King Lear*, ed. Kenneth Muir, Cambridge, MS: Harvard University Press.

Shakespeare, William (1986), *The Sonnets and A Lover's Complaint*, ed. John Kerrigan, London: Penguin Books.

Simmel, Georg (1950), 'The Metropolis and Modern Life', in *Sociology of Georg Simmel*, ed. and trans. Kurt H. Wolff, New York: Macmillan Publishing, pp. 409–26.

Sinclair, Iain (2015), *London Overground*, London: Hamish Hamilton.

Stephen, Leslie (1948), 'In Praise of Walking', in *The Art of Walking*, ed. Edwin Valentine Mitchell, New York: The Vanguard Press, pp. 18–38.

Stevenson, Robert Louis (1946), *Virginibus Puerisque and Other Papers*, Harmondsworth: Penguin.

Stevenson, Robert Louis (2004), *Travels with a Donkey in the Cévennes*, ed. Christopher MacLachlan, London: Penguin.

Svevo, Italo (1987), *La Coscienza di Zeno e 'continuazioni'*, ed. Mario Lavagetto, Torino: Giulio Einaudi editore.

Tasso, Torquato (1962), *Aminta*. 5th ed., ed. Luigi Fassò, Firenze: G. C. Sansoni Editore.

Thoreau, Henry David (1982), 'Walking', in *The Natural History Essays*, Salt Lake City: Peregrine Smith Books, pp. 93–136.

Traherne, Thomas (1965), *The Poetical Works of Thomas Traherne*, ed. Gladys I. Wade, New York: Cooper Square Publishers.

Tranter, Rhys (2018), *Beckett's Late Stage: Trauma, Language, and Subjectivity*, Stuttgart: ibidem-Verlag.

Tucker, David (2012), *Samuel Beckett and Arnold Geulincx*, London: Continuum.

Van Hulle, Dirk (2006), 'Samuel Beckett's *Faust* Notes', *Samuel Beckett Today/ Aujourd'hui*, 16, pp. 283–97.

Van Hulle, Dirk (2009), 'Preface', in Samuel Beckett: *Company, Ill Seen Ill Said, Worstward Ho, Stirring Still*, ed. Dirk Van Hulle, London: Faber and Faber, pp. vii–xviii.

Van Hulle, Dirk and Mark Nixon (2013), *Samuel Beckett's Library*, Cambridge: Cambridge University Press.

Van Hulle, Dirk and Pim Verhulst (2017a), *The Making of Samuel Beckett's 'Malone meurt'/'Malone Dies'*, London: Bloomsbury.

Van Hulle, Dirk and Pim Verhulst (2017b), *The Making of Samuel Beckett's 'En attendant Godot'/'Waiting for Godot'*, London: Bloomsbury.

Van Hulle, Dirk and Shane Weller (2017), *The Making of Samuel Beckett's 'Fin de partie'/'Endgame'*, London: Bloomsbury.

Veit, Carola (2009), *Kraft der Melone: Samuel Beckett im Kino*, Berlin: Deutsche Kinematek – Museum für Film und Fernsehen.

Wallace, Anne (1993), *Walking, Literature and English Culture*, Oxford: Oxford University Press.

Walser, Robert (1985), *Der Spaziergang, Prosastücke und Kleine Prosa*, ed. Jochen Greven, Frankfurt: Suhrkamp Verlag.

Weller, Shane (2010), 'Adorno's Notes on *The Unnamable*', *Journal of Samuel Beckett Studies*, 19:2, pp. 179–95.

Whelan, Feargal (2021), 'The Permanent Way: Movement and Stasis in Beckett's Railways', in Galina Kiryushina, Einat Adar and Mark Nixon (eds), *Samuel Beckett and Technology*, Edinburgh: University of Edinburgh Press, pp. 29–43.

White, Edmund (2001), *The Flâneur: A Stroll through the Paradoxes of Paris*, New York: Bloomsbury.

Whitman, Walt (1996), *The Complete Poems*, ed. Francis Murphy, London: Penguin.

Wittgenstein, Ludwig (1984), *Werkausgabe*, vol. 1: *Tractatus Logico-Philosophicus, Tagebücher 1914–1916*, 'Anmerkungen über die Logik', *Philosophische Untersuchungen*, Frankfurt: Suhrkamp Verlag.

Wordsworth, Dorothy (1991), *The Grasmere Journals*, ed. Pamela Woof, Oxford: Oxford University Press.

Wordsworth, William (1952), *The Poetical Works of William Wordsworth*, Volume Two, 2nd ed., ed. Ernest. de Sélincourt, Oxford: Oxford University Press.

Wordsworth, William (1954), *The Prelude, with a Selection from the Shorter Poems, the Sonnets, the Recluse and the Excursus*, ed. Carlos Baker, New York: Holt, Rinehart and Winston.

Wordsworth, William (1971), *The Prelude. A Parallel Text*, ed. James C. Maxwell, London: Penguin.

*for Todd Hopkins, Brian Jones and
Anne McMonagle*

Cambridge Elements ☰

Beckett Studies

Dirk Van Hulle

University of Oxford

Dirk Van Hulle is Professor of Bibliography and Modern Book History
at the University of Oxford and director of the Centre for Manuscript Genetics
at the University of Antwerp.

Mark Nixon

University of Reading

Mark Nixon is Professor of Modern Literature and Beckett Studies at the University of
Reading and the Co-Director of the Beckett International Foundation.

About the Series

This series presents cutting-edge research by distinguished and emerging scholars,
providing space for the most relevant debates informing Beckett studies as well as
neglected aspects of his work. In times of technological development, religious
radicalism, unprecedented migration, gender fluidity, environmental and social crisis,
Beckett's works find increased resonance. Cambridge Elements in Beckett Studies is
a key resource for readers interested in the current state of the field.

Cambridge Elements ☰

Beckett Studies

For EU product safety concerns, contact us at Calle de José Abascal, 56–1°, 28003 Madrid, Spain or eugpsr@cambridge.org.

www.ingramcontent.com/pod-product-compliance
Ingram Content Group UK Ltd.
Pitfield, Milton Keynes, MK11 3LW, UK
UKHW020746200325
456518UK00006B/355